MW01134558

Who Are We?

Arthur Cromarty

Cover layout and design by:

William Fraser Advertising
www.wfadvertising.com

@TheTop Publications
3705 Arctic Blvd. St. 1508
Anchorage, Alaska 99503
www.atthetoppublications.com

Published by @TheTop Publications 8/12/2011

ISBN: 978-1-4389-1752-8 (sc)

Printed in the United States
Anchorage, Alaska

This book is printed on acid free paper.

Chapters

WHO ARE WE?
By Arthur Cromarty

This is a true-life documentation and analysis of black society in Alaska. Most of which comes from my life, the lives of my peers, and the lives of friends both white and black. There is a serious problem in our society and no one seems to want to properly address it. This isn't a book to speak down on white people or any particular race of people. No, never that. My race has been put down and misrepresented for centuries, I know how it feels. My intentions in this fictional series is to enlighten other races on who we are and to show us as blacks to understand "WHO ARE WE?" So I would like to thank you for lending me your thoughts and I hope you enjoy.

DEDICATED
IN LOVING MEMORY
OF

ARTHUR O. CROMARTY
SR.
&
SADIE R. CROMARTY

THE BLACK MAN

Misunderstood, underrated, envied, and hated the black man is by far the backbone of the black community. This is a bold but true statement that some of us realize and others choose to ignore. You see, as a man of any race, it is always important to display excellence in his community, because in his community the women, children, and elders are always watching him. That is why the black community is suffering as a whole. Centuries of oppression, disgrace, and humiliation has left black men torn from their duties as the backbone. "Humiliated?" Yes humiliated! What else do you call a man of or properly provide for his family? Don't fall for that talk about this is America and everybody has the same chance. America has only been allowing black men to be educated since 1900's. They are strong and intelligent by nature but weak and ignorant by design.

The only thing we as black people have to call true heritage is slavery, poverty, and oppression. That explains the poor morals under which most of us operate y still to this day. For instance, if you have a society of educated scholars, businessmen, land thieves, murderers, and warlords the chances of having a similar society hundreds of years in the future is very possible. It's their heritage. Therefore a society of slaves, slaves, and more slaves could very well produce a free society of people with enslaved minds hundreds of years later. This is what it means to be black in America. Black meaning our culture and way of life, not skin color. You can't look at me and see a black man, black means how I live, dress, maintain, and eat. Some black people choose to be African-Americans even though the only ties we have with Africans is our skin color.

Africans have a culture and history that dates back thousands of years. Blacks in America, Haitians, Dominicans, etc have culture and history that dates back no further than slave ships carrying horrified passengers far from their place of origin. And like a mythical tale, emerged a new race of humans, adapting to a new land, food source, and torture. These strong men and women survived with hopes that future generations would have a better life than the their predecessors. Oppressed, exploited, and left with the white man's table scraps from the darkest chapter in world history, we survived.

"Domino muthafucka," yelled Sean as he slams his last domino onto the table.

"What the fuck," said Rico in utter frustration! "Can't you stop this muthafucka from scoring?"

"Bullshit," replied Jerome! "I don't see you doing much to stop him."
"My partner got you muthafuckas arguing with each other," said Paul pausing to slam double five on the loosely structured folding table. "That's game!"

"Get yall stanky asses up," replied Sean as he throws his dominos back on the table! Paul laughs with the intensions to taunt Jerome and Rico.

"Me and Carl got next," said Henry but Carl having being beaten all night, doesn't want to play anymore.

"Carl, why are you so quiet," asked Sean? "Janet been kicking yo ass again?"

"You know you better be getting home before Janet comes looking for yo ass," added Paul.

Everyone in the room laughed as Carl takes the center of attention away from the two who just lost the last game. Carl is the youngest of the men in the room so he is used to teasing that all the older guys throw at him. At the same time he's always protected by his brother-in-law Sean and his big brother Paul. Although Carl is grown up, to Sean and Paul he's still little brother.

"Fuck some dominos," blurted out Henry . "Somebody needs to go to the liquor store because this is the last drink." With one eye closed staring down the neck of an empty cognac bottle with that bad drinker face. Henry was a tall, slender guy in his late thirties. He was always clean cut and nicely dressed. Henry was also the heaviest drinker in the group.

"Damn nigga, that's all yo ass do is drink," said Paul.

"You need to be drinking too," replied Rico. "I know you didn't get away from your woman tonight just for yo ass to be sitting there drinking Pepsi. That goes for all yall brothers."

"Speak for yourself," says Jerome "I'm single." Jerome was the rudest and most belligerent of the group with a real hatred towards all women. Although he's not the best looking guy, ironically the ladies love Jerome.

"I'm not drinking cause I gotta work in the morning," replied Paul. Paul was a slim, light-brown skinned man that most women find to be rather attractive. He also shares the same single status as Jerome but he's a lot nicer to the ladies. And yes, Paul does have a lot of "lady friends."

"I bet you wanna hit this broken arm I got here," said Carl referring to the huge joint that he had just pulled from behind his ear.

"Hell yeah," replied Paul, Jerome, and Rico.

"Here man blaze," said Carl as he threw the joint to Sean.

"Are you going to hit it Henry," asked Jerome?
"Hell no," replied Henry! "You know I don't chief."

"Give it here I'll take his hit," said Paul.

"Hey man yall fucking up the rotation," says Rico as

Like this evening before I left the house, Janet was talking some shit about a stripper being here tonight. Like every time I get with the homies, we fucking with bitches."

"Damn," replied Sean! "She really does be on some crazy, jealous shit huh?"

"Man I don't know how much of this I can take," replied Carl. "It's like she drives me crazy with all the nagging and shit. I want to be with her just without all the constant bitching."
"The only cure for that shit is bachelorism," said Sean as he looked at Carl, laughing with an ice-melted, watered-down drink. "Besides she can barely speak English, just act like you can't understand her and ignore her ass."

"Easy for you to say Sean," replied Carl.

"I know," laughed Sean "my wife is black and can speak English."

"Fuck you man," laughed Carl "pass me the joint."

"Look at Henry's drunk ass," said Sean. "He's always attracting drunk broads cause they got something in common. Rico is always starting some shit that's why he always attract women with drama. And let's not forget your brother. Paul is a die hard bachelor. That's why he always has a new flavor of the month."

"Yeah, that's my brother," inserted Carl "find-em, fuck-em, and flee."

"That's our brother," said Sean. "That's why I'm with Evette, she's my everything. I like kicking it with the fellows but me and Evette can kick it just the same. She's my best friend, my lover, my family, and my babies-mama. We share a bond with each other that dates back as far as childhood and a love that seems to last as long as our hearts are able to conceive the emotion of love. You see, Jerome on the other hand, wants to be like me and Evette he just makes fucked up choices in women. He thinks having a pussy makes you a good woman."

"You can say that shit again," interrupted Carl as he reached for the joint. "Nigga yo ass act like you are a psychologist on relationships or some shit. Damn, Dr. Phil."

"You can't teach a young muthafucka nothing," laughed Sean.

Carl just ignores Sean as he gazed through the sliding glass doors on the balcony looking in on the other guys talking and laughing on the inside. He paused and tuned Sean out for a second to reflect on his own relationship with Janet and swallowed the guilt he felt deep inside for his recent actions. He know he couldn't consult Sean because Sean's best friend Bruce was at the center of it all.

"Come on, let's go back inside," suggested Sean as he swallows the last gulp of cognac and cola from his glass. "I'm thirsty!"

"Sean, will you tell your brother-in-law that the white girl he brought to the last barbecue was a ho," Rico blurted at Sean as Carl and he re-entered the house from the balcony. That was Rico's way of trying to get Sean to co-sign his attempt to start some shit.

Come on with that shit Rico," replied Sean looking at Carl out of the corner of his eye confirming what he had told him earlier on the balcony about Rico being a shit starter. "We got together tonight to chill, don't start that shit. Besides, he among you without a white girl in his past or present, may he cast the first stone."

Sean and Rico explode into laughter as everyone else shake their heads pleading no contest.

Although all the men in the room are close, Sean sometimes feels distant from the other guys because he and his best friend Bruce are the only ones who finds an interest in black women. Paul dates lots of women but it just so happens that none of them have ever been black. Jerome is older than the other guys and more experienced in life but he always chooses to stay neutral in racial discussions because his ex-wife is white. They all use the excuse that they can't control who they fall in love with but they mostly date white women.

"Man fuck a black bitch," says Rico as he downs a shot of cognac! "All black women do is complain about shit and stay in yo pockets. Bitch get a job! White girls be having they own money and don't complain like these nagging ass black hos."

"Rico don't make me rip yo ass from behind that bar," growled Sean clinching his fist to the point of cracking knuckles and veins bulging from his neck and forearms!

"Yall need to chill on that shit," said Henry.

"Rico why would you say some shit like that," asked Jerome?

"Man Sean, you can't get mad at me cause you are stuck with a black woman," inserted Rico.

"That is why we get together every week," added Henry "to talk as men and speak what's on our minds without the women around."

"Calm down Sean," says Paul. "It's still Rico he's just drunk. Don't let it get to you."
"That muthafucka always gets drunk and says some fucked up shit like that," screamed Sean as Carl tries to get him to the door. "Get your damn hands off me Carl unless you want some too!"

"Man you talking crazy Sean, we're all homies in here," says Carl. "Calm down brother."

"Carl how can you talk, Janet don't speaka noa muthafucking engrish," said Sean as he grabbed his coat and headed for the door. "Everyone in this room except Carl has a black daughter and yall let this muthafucka say fuck a black bitch! All yall niggas some hos!"

Sean storms out the front door and everyone let of a sigh of relief.

As Sean storms down the stairs from Rico's condo he runs into Duane getting out of his truck. Duane was Carl's best friend and he was coming to party with his friends until he ran into Sean. Duane was always late because he worked all the time. He owns his on plumbing company and it consumed all his time. All the men are highly paid professionals and business owners. They don't fit the stereotypes because money was no issue to these men.

"What's up wit it Sean," asked Duane approaching Sean with a fifth of cognac in both hands at the same time noticing that Sean really seemed pissed.

"Hey man, come and run me to my guy's crib," said Sean "I need to clear my head."

"What the fuck Sean, I just got here Sean," replied Duane. "I'm ready to get my drink on."

"I'm talking about Bear homie," said Sean smiling at Duane.

"Oh say no more, let's go nigga," responded Duane because he knows that Bear has the best weed in Anchorage. They jumped back Duane's truck and backed out of the driveway.

"Bring some more liquor back," yelled Henry from the upstairs balcony!

"What the hell is Henry yelling about," asked Duane?

"Fuck him," replied Sean scrolling through his list of numbers in his cell phone looking for Bear's number. Duane drove away.

Meanwhile back upstairs in Rico's condo, the other guys laugh and joke about all the times that Sean has gotten pissed off and stormed out of their get-togethers. The fact of the matter is that no matter how hostile the whole incident may seem, all of these guys love each other like brothers. Even though they all originated from the southern United States, all they have is each other in Alaska. Sean is bigger and stronger than the other guys but he would never harm his brothers. He loved them all no matter what their views were or who they dated.

"Henry who did Sean leave with," asked Paul?

"It looked like Duane's or Bruce's truck but I couldn't really tell," answered Henry.

"Yo Paul, what's up wit Maggie," asked Paul? "I thought she was a keeper."

"Man I had to leave that brawd alone," replied Paul. "She was psycho. I'd get home for work and this bitch would be parked in my driveway sleep talking about she's been there all day waiting for me to get off work. Then she start showing up at my job to bring me lunch but the problem with that was I never told her where I worked."

Everyone laughed furiously!

"Then she would invite me over to her place for dinner," Paul continued "I get there and this woman was cooking all tree-hugger food. Man she had a lot of money but it wasn't enough to put up with her shit. I only hit it one time and she lost her damn mind."

"That nigga a damn lie," inserted Jerome "he was fucking that brawd everyday."

"Bullshit," blurted Paul!
"Me and Henry came to you house twice when she was there," said Jerome "and you wouldn't bring yo punk-ass to the door."

"Jerome you better leave my brother alone," said Carl. "We aint gone mention that crazy bitch you had that broke in your house while you were sleep. Then you woke up and this brawd was standing over yo ass crying."

They all laughed!

"Man that shit wasn't funny," replied Jerome. "She kept getting in, I'd change all the locks and she'd still get in."

"This is my house," added Rico "I wish a muthafucka would break in here."

"We all know you like those kind of women," said Paul as everyone continued to laugh at each others relationship follies.

Rico has three kids in Texas but he doesn't get along with their mother so he won't pay child support. Like Rico she is a lawyer and doesn't need the money but she wants to cause Rico problems. They met in law school and after having two kids, Rico leaves her in the middle of the night while she was sleeping headed for Alaska. She has tried to make his life hell every since. Henry has a boy and a girl. He takes good care of them as a single dad. Although his ex-wife is a crackhead and well known in the drug community, she occasionally tries to be a mother.

Carl finds all their problems and relationships to be amusing. His relationship with Janet is pretty solid except for her constant nagging and his guilt for what he had done recently. For the most part they appeared to be a pretty solid young couple.

"Rico this is your crib," said Henry "you should go get some more cognac."

"Man didn't you tell Sean to bring some back," asked Rico? "Chill yo ass the fuck out you alcoholic."
"Man yall want to go to the Lovely Lady," asked Paul as he pulls out another joint? "We can get some drinks at the club after we smoke this joint."

"Man yall always smoking that shit," said Henry as he lights up a cigarette.

"Carl get the door," says Rico responding to a knock at the door.

"Who do I look like? Benson in this muthafucka," sarcastically asked Carl as he fumbled with the deadbolt?

"Hurry up and open the door before I kick that shit in," yells Bruce from the other side of the door! "What's up wit it," said Bruce as he entered the door with more weed and cognac. "Where's my man Sean at? Don't tell me he already got pissed off and left."

"Yep," everybody replied while laughing!

"Who was that at the door," yelled Rico from his bedroom where he was rolling more joints.

he reaches for his own weed stash to roll a joint also.

As all the fellows argue back and forward about who has the best weed, the best spot to go clubbing, and what bartender has the fattest ass, Carl noticed Sean standing alone on the balcony. Over looking the city with his back turned towards everyone inside choking due to the lungs full of weed smoke he had just inhaled. Sean is a handsome, brown skinned man that owns a logging camp and works it as well with the muscles and ripples to show for it. Sean is also well respected among the guys and he shows everyone around him respect. Not only is he married to Paul and Carl's sister Evette, but all the guys are close friends like brothers.

"What's going on Sean," asked Carl as he steps out onto the balcony closing the door behind himself? "Why are you out here by yourself?"

"Fresh air," replied Sean "fresh air. I like smoking weed like the next man but that cigarette smoke is burning my eyes. Tell them to send that joint out here. I was smoking a roach."

"Nall that's okay, I got another one right here," replied Carl as he lit a second joint, bellowing smoke into the air like a black dragon with braids. "Why have you been so quite tonight? Have you and Evette been arguing or something? Don't let that shit spoil our night. She's my big sister but women in general on a constant nagging trip.

"It's me," responded Bruce. Bruce is also close to Sean because they grew up together hustling and selling dope while they paid their ways through college. Sean got serious with Evette after college and had kids. He started his own business, not risking going to jail and leaving his wife and kids behind, but not Bruce. Bruce was still up to the same thing. He also has a wife and kids but Bruce is a thug for life. He has more cash, cars, and houses than all the other guys put together.

"Jerome I'm riding with you," said Henry.

"Where yall getting ready to go," asked Bruce?

"The Lovely Lady," Paul quickly responded.

"That's what I'm talking about the strip club," said Bruce pulling out a knot of hundreds and fifties so thick they can't even fold.

"We are waiting for Rico to roll those joints," said Jerome.
"Say man, did you ever get rid of that psycho brawd," asked Bruce?

"Aww fuck, now here you go," replied Jerome!

"I'm just fucking wit ya," chuckled Bruce. "Rico hurry yo ass up. You know if we don't get there before them project niggas all the good looking girls go home.

"Like them hos wanna see yo ugly ass," Carl said jokingly.

"Shiiiit! That muthafucka got cold cash," said Paul. "That nigga looks like a model to them hos."

"Man fuck both yall niggas," responded Bruce!

Rico walks out of the back room with a joint in his mouth and a shirt pocket with four blunts.

"Where in the hell you been hiding," asked Rico as he shakes hands with Bruce?

"Just chilling and stacking my paper," replied Bruce. "You know me."

"I saw your old lady the other day at Safeway, she acted like she couldn't even speak," says Henry.

"I know, she been tripping lately," replied Bruce. "I think she's fucking some nigga in Mt. View but you know black women. They'll deny that shit to the end. That's why I told Michelle last night to go give that nigga some pussy cause she damn sure not getting none from me."

Everybody laughs!

"After you let another man touch you it's over," added Bruce. "I don't want that shit no more. "You dig?"

At that moment Sean and Duane walks through the door without knocking. Both of them carrying fifths of cognac and twelve packs of beer. Sean seemed to be relaxed after the incident earlier, thanks to a fresh ounce of the sweetest smelling ganja from Bear's personal stash. Followed by Duane greeting and shaking everyone's hand.

"Where the fuck yall going after I went out and bought all this liquor," asked Sean looking around the room at everyone. Then he pulled out an ounce of Alaska's finest weed. "Not to mention we just left Bear's crib."

"We are supposed to be going to the Lovely Lady......," Henry replied but he was quickly interrupted.

"Put this cognac in the cabinet and let's go," said Sean before Henry could finish his sentence then walked over to Bruce and whispered "we need to talk."
"Come on niggas, let's go," said Henry as everyone walked out the door arguing about who was driving.

"Man your ass is forever losing shit," said Sean as he watched Rico franticly look for his keys. "You would lose your dick if it wasn't tied up with yo nuts."

"Yeah, very funny," replied Rico, pausing then laughing out loud!

"Hey man, no hard feelings Rico, we are supposed to be having a good time, right," says Sean with his hand extended out to Rico.

The two men shake hands and hug with the certainty of friendship and the reassurance of family.

"Still brothers," says Rico.

"Still brothers," replied Sean.

"C'mon man, you two muthafuckas need to hurry up with that ol' friendly ass shit," interrupted Carl as he burst back in the door. "I wanna see some titties shaking and ass clapping!"

THE BLACK WOMAN

Six women laughing and talking gathered around a pool on a roof top overlooking whole city from the Anchorage hillside. They sip on expensive wine while they play a game of spades under the bright Alaskan sun. There is a slight hint of weed in the air but not near as much as the men.

"It's your partners turn, whenever she brings her ass out of the bathroom," said Sharon. A heavyset black woman with beautiful hair and a very charming character. Sharon was the female version of Rico.

"Don't worry about my partner, she got some spades," replied Monica.

"Yeah like the spade around her eye," said Sharon in a low tone!

"Oooohh," responded Monica!

Melissa and Evon start laughing while lounging by the pool.

"Don't start," inserted Evette. A dark skinned female with super model qualities. Thick and curved in all the right places. Small and slim everywhere else with flawless skin.

" All I'm saying is why she won't take off those

shades," replied Sharon? "I grew up with seven brothers, I aint scared, we can go kick his ass. Don't be putting your hands on my girl!

"Shhh, here she comes," said Monica!

"Bitch don't be shhh-ing me, you crazy," snapped Sharon laughing and high-fiving with Evette as Michelle sits down at the table without a clue of what the conversation was about!

"Sharon what happened with that fine ass chocolate man you left the club with last night," asked Evon being the peacemaker in the group sensing a need to quickly change the subject?

"Ooooo girl, you aint going to believe this shit," replied Sharon as everyone moved to the edge of their seats, anticipating what she was going to say!

"Girl did you get you some cause that's all we want to hear," asked Evette insinuating that Sharon not get into one of her freaky tales adventures.?

"No, wait a minute, I'm going to get to that part," responded Sharon. "First I'm going to let yall know he was like a worthless baseball player because he struck out quick. The first strike was when we left the club nether one of us wanted to drive so we agreed on a cab. When the cab gets to my house, he aint got the money to pay for the cab."
"Whaaat," laughed Melissa!

"Damn," gasped Evon in disbelief!

"I know, aint that a bitch," replied Sharon! "So then we get down to it, you know cutting through the chase. I'm in the bed naked, he unbuckles his pants and the biggest, blackest dick I ever seen flopped out."

"Girl are you lying," asked Monica?

"Did you notice I said it flopped out, okay," answered Sharon! "Then all of a sudden (sniffing), damn that's strike two! I smell salty onions and ass. This nigga should know that with a dick that big you should wash daily. Especially before you go to the club."

"What the fuck," frowned Evette!

"Then he goes into the bathroom," continued Sharon "so I'm thinking he must have smelled himself and went to wash up right. Maybe he was clean and got sweaty at the club from dancing. Then I look over on the floor and saw strike three. Shity drawers on the floor!"

"Eeewww," screamed Melissa and Evon!

"I think I'm gonna be sick," replied Michelle as she shivered in her seat.
"I know you didn't give him none," asked Evette as she squinted her face?

"Hell no," snapped Sharon! "I snatched all the linen off the bed, put a towel between my legs, and when he came out the bathroom I told him my period just came on. I'm sorry bruh but you gots to go!"

"Ha ha ha," everyone laughed hysterically!

"Sharon that is fucking sick," said Evette. "I just want you to know."

"Girl that was the only thing I could think of that would turn a man off real quick," replied Sharon.

"His friend was trying to pick me up but I don't fall for pick up lines. A man would stand a better chance with me by just being themselves," said Melissa.
"I agree," added Evon "pick up lines are a sign of immaturity."

Melissa goes to change the CD in the stereo as she wondered how long they could keep Sharon off the subject of Michelle's black eye. Sharon was a shit-starter and it was only a matter of time.

"Hey Evette," asked Monica "what's up with your fine ass little brother? You know he's old enough for me to teach him some tricks!"

"Monica you better leave my little brother alone," responded Evette. "Besides he's all rapped up in Janet and he aint thinking about nobody else."

"Oh yeah that's right, Janet," replied Monica in a sarcastic tone!

"Janet hmm," says Evon sitting in her pool chair with her head bent down looking over her shades.

"Don't get no ideas," said Evette "cause he is happy and I want home to stay that way. Besides I don't want him hooking up with nether on of you freaky hos. Evon you're into white boys anyway."

"I know she didn't," quickly responded Evon in disbelief.

Michelle and Sharon laugh out loud!

"So what are you saying Evette," asked Monica?

"Both yall go through men like....," Evette started to say and then paused. "All I'm saying is he's a grown man and yall are my friends but just not him."

"I'm not that freaky I just like to do it," inserted Monica.

"Come on Evon, be more specific," blurted Sharon "you like to do white men."
"What's wrong with white men," asked Monica?

"What's right with them," asked Evette?

"I'll give any man a chance that'll treat me good and make me feel romantic," inserted Evon. "Who cares what color he is? "Most black men just wanna hit it, they don't want to be romantic. That's why I date white guys."

"Listen to what you just said," inserted Evette "you only date white men. If you are looking for love and romance, why do you feel Black, Asian, or Spanish men don't possess these qualities."
"You still have to date and spend time with a white guy just to find out if he has those qualities," added Sharon. "I can't get over that hump."

"Yall act like it's something wrong with it," said Monica. "Besides all the brothers are dating white women."

"Hmmm," responded Evette and Sharon with a whatever sigh!

"Melissa what do you think," asked Michelle as Melissa laughed at the whole conversation?

"I think Evette and Sharon are right but Monica and Evon have the right to date who ever they want," replies Melissa. "I guess I have mixed emotions about it. Maybe because my dad is black and my mom is white."
"That's why I'm glad I'm married so I don't have to deal with that type of drama," said Michelle while shaking her head.

"Drama," yelled Sharon right on cue as everyone anticipated a strong and vulgar response from her. "Bitch I know you didn't say nothing about drama with all the ass whippings you be taking from Bruce. That's probably why you won't take those shades off now. I told you before that I would help you kick his ass. I got your back, you still my girl I just think you're stupid for staying with him."

"If you are really my friend, how could you suggest I leave my husband," asked Michelle with tears rolling down her face from behind her shades? "Take my kids away from their farther? Really Sharon, is that being a friend?"

"Michelle you need to calm down," said Evette smacking her beautiful lips! "Sharon is normally just starting shit but I agree with her on this one. You can't be letting a muthafucka pound on you, especially when your kids are around."

"No, you calm down Evette," promptly responded Michelle!

"We are just trying to talk some sense into you," interrupted Sharon!

"I'm always listening to my friends," cried Michelle! "I just want my friends to let me talk for once. I really do love my husband and he loves me. We are happy together, it's just that right now we are having some problems that's all. I'm not leaving my husband! The only reason he hits me is because I always push him to the limit when we argue but Bruce is good to me."

"This bitch is sillier than I thought," laughed Sharon! "Well as long as you like it, I love it. With yo silly ass!"

"I just hope yall get that shit under control," added Evette. "If not for yourself, at least for the kid's sake. They don't need to see momma getting her ass kicked."

"Hmmm," sighed Evon in disbelief as if she knows something the other ladies don't know!

Melissa and Monica walk over to give Michelle a hug for support while Evette and Sharon look at each other rolling their eyes.

"All this sympathy talk is making my pussy ache," said Evon carelessly as she walks back into the house. "I'll be in the sauna if anybody needs me."

"What's gotten into Evon," asked Melissa?

"I can't believe she just did that," said Evette "she act like it's nothing."
"Oh hell nah," shouted Sharon as she jumps out of her seat to go after Evon!

"Hold on, this is my house Sharon," as she jumps up

from her own seat in order to short stop Sharon. "If anybody is finna start some shit it's going to be me!"

"What are you two doing," asked Monica? "That's just Evon being Evon."

"Monica is right, maybe Evon is just upset about taking that job in Seattle," blurted out Melissa!

"Shhh," grunted Monica while smacking her lips!

Everyone goy quite for a few seconds that seemed like an eternity.

"What job in Seattle," asked Evette breaking the silence?

"That bitch was going to move to Seattle and not tell us," asked Sharon?

"I'm sure she had intentions on telling everybody, so let's not jump to conclusions," said Monica.

"Well, how in the fuck do yall bitches know and we don't," asked Evette?

"Maybe she don't know how to tell us," said Sharon.

"Maybe that was her way of telling everybody, first tell big mouth," said Monica referring to Melissa "and then the whole city will know."

"Is she really leaving," asked Sharon?
"Maybe she's just confused," added Evette.

"I'm gonna go talk to her," said Sharon as she walks towards the sliding glass doors.

"Sharon," everyone blurted out at once!

"I said I'm going to talk to her," replied Sharon as she entered the house. "Damn! Yall act like I'm gone fight the girl!"

"I hope she does leave," responded Michelle as she removes her shades, exposing her bruised yet watery eyes.

"What are you saying Michelle," asked Monica?
"Evon is all of our friend."

"I'm sorry, I shouldn't be saying shit like that but I have my reasons for being salty," replied Michelle as she continued to cry.

"What's going on," simultaneously asked Monica and Melissa as the moved their chairs closer to Michelle?

"Well I'm not a hundred percent sure," said Michelle " so you guys have to promise not to say anything until I find out the truth."

"Will you just spit it out already," suggested Evette.

"What is it?"

"Well about six weeks ago," Michelle started to explain, "I started to feel like Bruce was acting kind of strange. You know, like he's seeing somebody kind of strange. For the first two weeks it seemed to get more and more obvious. So four weeks ago I hired a private detective just to follow him around and see what he is up to. Then it turned out to be true. He was seeing somebody else. So the private detective offered to take pictures, of course it was in an attempt to get more money but what the hell I accepted. He brought me pictures from bars, parks, coffee shops, etc."

"All those places you named where they met could be friendly," interrupted Evette. "Those are all public places. It could be harmless."

"That's true," added Melissa.

"Well that's not all," said Michelle as she continued to explain. "When he brought the pictures to me, every one of them were pictures of Bruce and Evon!"

There was complete silence for no one could respond. Meanwhile inside the house Sharon tries to figure out what was wrong with Evon.
"Michelle is still my girl but she's fowl and I'm caught up in the middle of her shit," said Evon with anger in his voice!

"Bitch don't play just tell me," replied Sharon.

"You have to prom….," Evon started to say but was rudely interrupted by Sharon.

"I'm not promising shit," strongly stated Sharon! "Just tell me what shit it is you are in the middle of."

"Well lately I've been playing counselor," Evon started to explain with the burning desire to tell someone her secret. "Now I don't know why he picked me but Bruce started asking me about a month ago to meet him places. At first it was just to ask me questions about Michelle, like if she was seeing anybody and stuff like that. Then when he found out who she was seeing he was heated and I was shocked my damn self."

"Who was it," anxiously asked Sharon?

"It doesn't matter, now she probably thinks I'm having an affair with her husband," replies Evon.

"As a friend you should tell her," says Sharon.

"But they're both my friends," responded Evon. "How do you keep both friends secret when you know each one should know the truth but to know the truth would crush both of them."

"Well tell me," pleaded Sharon. "who is she seeing?"

"Carl," said Evon in a low whisper.

"Carl," shouted Sharon!

"Shhh," signaled Evon.

"You mean Evette's little brother Carl," replied Sharon.

Evon didn't respond. Instead she took a deep breath and starred at the ceiling. Then after a brief pause, Sharon finally spoke with deep concern in her face, and in a soft whisper Sharon asked, "What's this I hear about a job in Seattle?"

"Oh Sharon, I don't know what to do," replied Evon with tears in her eyes. "I love all of yall but if I stay here and don't take the job I'll be passing up a good opportunity. What I really wanna do is stay here in Anchorage. I just feel that everyone is going to hate me after this whole Bruce situation, on top of me keeping this a secret from Evette. My friends will never look at my the same. So why not move to Seattle?"
"Come on girl, that's crazy," said Sharon! " We are your friends, if you try to explain they will listen. And if they listen, they will understand. Nobody is going to hate you or think less of you. But you can't keep this a secret, you have to tell everyone so they don't start to draw their own conclusions."

"I guess you're right," said Evon as she wiped the

tears from here face.

"And I can't get over Michelle, what the fuck is she thinking," replied Sharon as she walked towards the door. "This bitch is out there acting like she the victim. If Evette knew she was fucking Carl, she would throw her trifling ass over that balcony!"

"Sharon don't," blurted out Evon!

"Don't worry I'm not going to say nothing," replied Sharon turning around to face Evon, "but you do need to say something."

"Okay, I understand Sharon," smiled Evon "I'm going to have talk with everybody."

Sharon walked over to Evon to give her a hug and then went back outside on the patio.

THE COMMUNITY

As the small convoy of cars and trucks head to the Lovely Lady with a cloud of smoke following them down the street, Sean his truck accompanied by Bruce and Henry. Sean stops by the Carrs grocery store in Fairview to buy breath mints.

"Damn man, look at that brawd in them jeans in front of the store," blurted out Henry as Sean parks in front of the store!

"Damn he aint lying," said Sean! "That muthafucka is fine!"

Bruce doesn't look up because he is too busy scrolling through the numbers in his cell phone.

"Henry I need to talk to Bruce for a minute," said Sean. "Do you mind going in the store for the gum?"

"Yeah it's cool I have to buy some cigarettes anyway," replied Henry as he opened the door to get out of the truck. "Yall see that brawd right, watch me put my mack down. She's in my grasp already and don't even know it."

"Let's see you go to work then playa," added Bruce smiling. "I got fifty that says you don't pull her."

"Bet," says Henry as he quickly jumps out of the truck to avoid giving Bruce a chance to back out of the bet!

"Say brother you could have saved your money," Sean laughed, "because you are going to lose that bet. She's a white girl and he is a successful black business owner. Automatic match maker in her eyes. She aint got know job, she broke, and she probably got some mixed babies with fucked up hair cause she can't do it. But she is white and that's all she need to catch most of these niggas."

"Nigga you sick wit it," chuckled Bruce. "And how in the hell do you know she aint got know job?

"If she did she wouldn't be hanging out in front of the store at this time of night," replied Sean.

"I'm not against interracial fucking but I am against interracial marriage," added Bruce. "But I doubt if Henry got plans on getting married."

"Yeah, I guess you are right," smiled Sean, "some niggas will stick their dicks in anything."
Both of them laugh as Henry makes his way back to the truck.

"Look Bruce, don't ever doubt my skills son," says Henry as he hops back into the truck. "You can pay me later."

"You know pulling a white girl is not really considered a challenge," said Bruce.

"Ahh shit you couldn't have pulled that brawd if you tried," inserted Henry!

"Henry you got me fucked up," said Bruce. "Sean turn this muthafucka around, I'll go put it down on that brawd right now."

"Man I'm not turning around shit," replied Sean. "I can't believe you two muthafuckas are still betting and arguing over the same shit yall was betting and arguing about back in college."

"Don't be hating on us cause Evette revoked your playa card," said Bruce.

When they were all in college together Sean and Evette stopped dating for a while but Sean never was a player. He just dated a lot of women one at a time. Bruce has always been with Michelle, they have never been separated. Bruce has always just done whatever he wanted to do even in high school. Henry has been single as far back as anyone could remember. Most of the women that Henry dates are just like him, single and really wants to stay that way. The other guys see Henry and Rico as being very much alike. Both of them have a serious problem with commitment and monogamy.

"What did you want to talk to me about," asked Sean?
"I guess it's cool to talk about now, we are all homies," replies Sean.

"For sho," said Bruce "for sho."

"What's been going on with you and Michelle," asked Sean? "You know she always goes crying to Evette and I get stuck with the Sean you need to talk to yo boy speech."

"Everything is cool, we are just having some problems like any other couple," responded Bruce. "She's been up to some shit lately but I'm not gonna put my hands on her no more. I'm done. At this point I just want my kids and my barber shop, she can have everything else."

"Damn, what the fuck is she doing that is so bad," asked Henry?

"That's what I want to know," said Sean.

"Well if you really want to know," said Bruce. "I'm pretty sure she's having an affair with your brother-in-law."

"Get the fuck outta here," said Sean! "Are you for real?"

"Which one," asked Henry?

"Carl," Bruce replied.
"CARL," yelled Sean and Henry as Sean almost runs his truck into the side of the club as they pull into the parking lot!

"Let me talk to him and find out what's going on,"

said Sean. "It may not be what you think."

"I wouldn't even sweat it if I were you," replied Bruce. "I'm just tired of Michelle and her shit anyway, I don't care what she does. It aint like I haven't had my share of women."

"But if what you are saying is true, they are both wrong," inserted Henry. "We are not talking about your wife cheating with the a stranger, we are talking about one of the homies."

"It's cool man," said Bruce, "it's cool."

"No Bruce," Sean replies "Henry is right. They are both out of order. Because out of all the women in this city, why would Carl want to mess with the homie's wife. And with all the men in this city, why would Michelle want to mess with one of her husband's homies? I'm just saying let me talk to him first. Now let's go in here and watch some ass shaking."

"Okay, let's go," said Bruce.

As the three men exit the vehicle they are confronted by some strange woman yelling and screaming about some black guy that raped her sister and got away with it. It was apparent to these men that she was drunk. All three men stop in their tracks as the intoxicated female gets closer and closer. About six feet from being in the mens faces, crying and screaming, she drops flat on her face asleep in the middle of the parking lot.

"What the fuck is wrong with that bitch," said Sean as the three men stepped over the apparently drunken lady laughing as hard as they could.

"Don't worry about her," says the bouncer at the door, a large Samoan man with braided hair. "She has been running up to every brother in the parking lot tonight saying that shit I called the police twice already, let her ass lie there. You gentlemen enjoy yourselves."

They all head into the club to join the rest of their friends sitting at a large table drinking. Paul knowing what everybody drinks already have drinks waiting for them on the table. All the dancers rush the table when they see Sean And Bruce walk in because they know that these two are regular customers and big spenders. Not saying that they blow money in the strip clubs but they got it like that. Bruce has a real lucrative cocaine business fronted by a barber shop and a cab company. Sean got hurt when he was younger at a logging camp in Oregon. It's rumored that he received a large lawsuit settlement and that's how he started his own logging camp in Northern Alaska. Plus he already had a lot of money before that so no one really knows how much Sean is worth. Sean is also suspected of being secret partners with Bruce. Although no one could understand why Bruce

went all the way through college and graduated just to deal cocaine. Henry, Jerome, and Paul also have a lot of money but most of their money was tied up in real estate ventures. Duane and Carl are younger, they're just into working hard. Like most young people their age, they have no desire to go to college. Then there's Rico. Rico was a lawyer that man-whored his way through law school.

"Hey daddy, where have you been? I haven't seen you in a while," said Passion. A dark-skinned, thick, well curved female that usually hand picks her clients by their tipping habits. She is a lot more sophisticated and refined than the other girls but she's still about her money.

"I've been busy," replied Bruce. He knows she's not the prettiest dancer in the club but she carries herself the best.

"Where is your friend," asked Sean? "You know, Sapphire."

"Damn nigga it's some fine bitches in here," rudely interrupted Jerome leaning over the table. "Why yall muthafuckas never told me about this spot?"

Of course with Carl and Duane being the youngest, they are the most rowdy but that doesn't matter to Jerome because he can get drunk and rowdy with the best of them. Paul and Rico kind of sit back and chill, enjoy the show sitting at the table across from

Bruce and Sean. Not Jerome, he was right up front flashing his dollars on the stage calling the dancers to himself in a disrespectful manner. Despite his insults, they still come his direction for the money.

Now Jerome has Duane and Carl on either side of him smacking the girl on stage on the ass with dollar bills. The girl on stage smile as if she is having fun but that is enough to convenience the guys to keep putting money on the stage. Everyone was having fun and enjoying the night. That's about the time when Janet and her cousin Christie walk in looking for Carl with an evil look on their faces.

"Oh shit, she's out of control for this shit," blurted out Paul as everybody notices them walk into the club!

"Yo Carl you've got to check her ass about this shit," said Jerome. "Nigga she came to this muthafucka to get yo ass. I know you aint gone let her get away with this shit."

Carl just sits there in disbelief as he listens to all the laughs and taunts in the background by Jerome and the rest of the fellows. If only he had a genie he could disappear from this situation. The most embarrassing thing for any man or woman to experience while hanging out with their friends is to have your mate come looking for you. Carl instantly blocks out the sound of everyone talking and the club speakers as if he's in an empty room alone with Janet. As she gets closer and closer he can feel the room getting smaller and smaller. Then the cold hard reality of her actually showing up at the club slowly sets in like arigamortis. His heart beats faster and faster, nostrils flare, shame and humiliation is evident. And despite the fact that his entire family is constantly advising him to get with a black woman, he was only at war with his emotions right now. Carl really loves Janet but his anger was overwhelming. He contemplates that maybe his family is right, as her stroll across the club to where he was sitting seemed like an eternity.

"Damn Janet, what the fuck," yelled Carl!

"Hey nigga, yo momma is here. Oops, I mean Janet," laughed Jerome in an attempt to instigate and worsen the situation!

"Fuck you Jerome," yells Janet as she throws her hand up in Jerome's face ignoring him while keeping her attention on Carl. "Am I not good enough for you? You have to be in here all up in these nasty bitches faces instead of spending time with me?"

"Janet, what in the hell are you talking about," asked Carl with a frown? "I'm with yo ass six days a week, I only chill with the homies one day. Sometimes we all need a break. Damn!"

"If you don't want to be with me that's fine," replied

Janet "but don't bring your drunk ass home. How about you go home with your homies!

"You're wrong for this shit Carl," interrupted Christie! "My cousin loves your black ass and you treat her like shit!"

"Hey bitch, you better watch yo mouth," inserted Duane!

"Bitch," repeated Christie shaking her head! "Who you calling bitch? Fuck you nigga!"

There was a brief moment of silence, then all hell would break loose. Everyone was yelling and screaming at each other. All you could hear was "fuck you this" and "punk bitch that"! The women were hurt and crying, and the men were offended and angry. It was safe to say at this point the situation was escalating fast. To make matters worse Duane was moving closer and closer towards Christie. That was about the time Sean stepped in and grabbed both Carl and Duane by the arm. Both men immediately jerked away from his grasp. Then about five bouncers approach the crowd.
"Whatever the problem is, yall gotta get out of here with that shit before I call the police," says the head bouncer!
Sean and Bruce look at each other knowing that they have a truck full of marijuana, rush to the front door without giving it a half of thought. Coming to their senses, everyone else soon follows. Disbursing

to their separate vehicles they could see Sean's truck crank and the lights come on.

"Where are yall going with all the gunja," yelled out Paul as Sean drove past?

"Getting the fuck outta here," replied Bruce!

"Everybody meet me back at my house," inserted Rico as he unlocked his car door.

Everyone acknowledged him and headed back to Rico's house. Sean was trying to drive carefully, constantly checking his rear view mirror as Bruce rolled more joints. They both look at each other as they get further and further away from the strip club, shaking their heads in disbelief. "Young niggas!" When they pulled into the parking lot of Rico's condo complex, Bruce noticed that no one else had made it back yet.

"Where is everybody at," asked Bruce? "Not good."

"It's cool, we'll just sit back and smoke one of those joints until they get here," replied Sean.

"That's right," responded Bruce "we do have all the gunja with us."
"Hello," said Sean as he answers his cell phone. Sean knew it was Carl from looking at the caller ID. "Yall niggas are stupid. I don't wanna hear it. And why

47

was Duane swelling up in the chest at Christie? If he would have touched that girl they would have locked both of yall black asses up. I don't agree with yalls relationship but she is still your baby's momma. Janet aint some random brawd."

"Don't tell those young muthafuckas nothing," added Bruce "let them learn the hard way if he wants to argue about it."

"I gotta go," says Sean as he watches a car park next to him and turn off the head lights. A white female jumps out of the car, walks up the stairs to Rico's front door, and starts pounding on the door. "I'll talk to you when you get here."

Bruce and Sean got out of the truck walked towards the female.

"Calm down girl, he aint here," said Bruce. "But you can wait for him in your car with all that noise." "This is not your house," the female replied "so fuck you!"

"Just respect my man's crib," said Sean! "He does have to live here!"

"Fuck you too," the female replied once again, directing her attention to Sean! "That nigga told me….."
CRACK!!! The woman drops to the ground like a wet rag doll as Bruce punches her in the mouth with no regard to her being a female.

"Stupid bitch," yells Bruce shaking his hand in the air looking for and stop to inspect his hand for broken skin! "What did she think was going to happen? It was gonna be cool to say nigga?"

"Don't blame her," replied Sean "blame Rico. "He must let her talk to him like that all the time because she seemed to be quite fluent with the word nigga. No hesitation at all. It happens all the time but what white and black people who think that shit is cool don't understand is that all black folks aint cool with that shit."

"Ya know," co-signed Bruce still rubbing his hand, checking for broken skin!

"Muthafuckas have been fighting and dying for years not to be called nigga," added Sean "but this dumb ass nigga got this white brawd calling him nigga."

"Rico is pretty fucking dumb to be a lawyer," laughed Bruce as they both stepped over the knocked out woman and walk back to the truck to finish smoking their blunt.

Meanwhile a second car pulls up, parks next to Sean's truck, and Rhonda steps out. Rhonda is not Rico's girlfriend but they have been seeing each other for years. Rhonda could be very jealous at times and this was one of those times. Sean and Bruce sparked up the blunt and got ready for the dramatic show that was about to take place. Sean passes the blunt to Bruce coughing and choking as they watch Rhonda's petite but well shaped frame get out of her car and walk over towards the white woman getting off the ground.

"Bitch I thought I told you to stay the fuck away from my man," yelled Rhonda quickening her pace!

"I'm not scared of you," the woman say as she shakes her head in a quick attempt to get it together. Just before Rhonda reaches her she makes a dash for her car. Rhonda makes chase, catches her by the back of the hair and starts pounding her face. Both women scratch, punch, kick, yell, and curse at each other until the neighbors start to turn on their lights and come outside.

"Rico better get here fast," laughed Sean.

"You should call him," added Bruce.

"I already did, his shit just keeps going to voice mail," replied Sean.

THE FAMILY

Early on a Saturday morning the Alaskan sun
shines bright, illuminating the Anchorage hillside
like a mountainous Christmas tree. Although it had
never gotten dark from the evening before there
was still morning dew and birds chirping. With no
plants or factories in this city surrounded by ocean
and mountains, Anchorage has the freshest morning
air in the world. Anchorage is a beautiful city but
the wealthier hillside residents always get to enjoy
breathe taking sunrises with the sun gracefully
dancing across the ocean. But outside of this one
luxurious hillside home, the peaceful morning
tranquility is interrupted by the sounds of marriage.

"Mhhh," sighed Evette as Sean softly plucks at her
nipples with his lips through her silky nightgown.

"Good morning Mrs. Banks," said Sean as he moves
up to her face and softly kisses her on the lips.
Evette smiled while she was being awakened by
her husbands romantic gesture to give her what she
wanted more than anything else. Morning sex!

"I love you too," responded Evette squirming her ass
around on the bed in anticipation.

"Mhhh Evette," whispered Sean "you have got to
be the sexiest woman on the planet!" Kissing her on
the neck and behind the ears while rubbing his rock
hard penis against her pelvis. She begins to squirm
deeper and faster.

"Damn baby, want to feel you inside me so bad," moaned Evette reaching down to grab his massive penis and rubs it up and down between the lips of her vagina!

"Hell yeah," grunted Sean as he thrust forward, pushing himself deep inside of her tight juicy hole!

"Ooh ooh," screamed Evette in total bliss feeling the walls of her vagina spread open as Sean shoved his entire penis deep inside her making a smacking sound. Sean started to thrust faster and deeper!

"Fuck yeah," grunted Sean!

"Oh shit," yelled Evette in complete ecstasy! "I'm gonna cum on your dick!"

Boom Boom Boom!

"The kids," they both blurted out in disappointment as Sean jumps out of bed scrambling for his pajama pants.
"Just a minute," says Sean as he walks towards the door and puts his ear to it. "What is it?"

"Dad, you said I can help you set up for the big day and today is the big day," yelled Sean Jr. from the other side of the door. It's just a barbecue but Sean Jr. always refers to it as the "big day" because he gets to see all his cousins and friends.

"I know Jr., I remember," replied Sean looking at his beautiful wife shaking his head in despair. "I'll be out in a minute, okay. Go and wake up your sisters."

"Dad I already did," replied Sean Jr. "I'm just waiting on you."

"Okay, here I come," said Sean.

"Come on Dad, hurry up," said Sean Jr.!

"Boy I said I'm coming," Sean replied with authority in his voice "don't be rushing me!"

"That's your son," added Evette.

"I'll get with you later," responded Sean then he turned and opened the door. "This is far from over."

Sean and Evette always hosted big family gatherings and functions at their house with the indoor/outdoor swimming pool and huge yard. Henry always worked the grill and by far he was the best at it. When Sean and Evette had their house built, they had a barbecue grill built into the patio just for Henry. They were a team because no matter who's house they were at, Sean always seasoned the meat and made side dishes. The two men together were one hell of a cooking combination. Evette and Sharon were the best at making kool-aid, iced tea, and mixed drinks. Rico was the best DJ and all of the children get along like family. It's almost like they all need each other to make a function or gathering successful. Them and their children are all so close to one another, they all just harmonized together. A strong self-made family unit with love and respect for each other most of the time but just like all families, they had their problems. At every family function you had to watch how much Henry has to drink before he finishes cooking on the grill. Sharon and Rico will tear away at each other's throat but whenever they played spades or dominoes, ironically they were always partners. Sean and Evette almost always sneak off to somewhere in their huge home to do the nasty. They had been into each other since college and they refused to let their love die. Like the couples of the old days, staying together no matter what life throws their way.

Sean and Sean Jr. seasoned and rubbed baby back ribs, pork chops, steaks, chicken, and Alaskan King Salmon. They also marinated shrimp and fresh vegetables for kabobs with lobster chunks wrapped with bacon. They ate like kings and queens at these family functions. Henry grilled ribeye steaks, bratwursts and burgers, beef briskets, hot dogs and hot links, porterhouses and pork shoulder. Then Sean and Evette would prepare dirty rice, boudins, mac and cheese, baked beans with ground beef and bacon, potato salad, corn on the cob, collard greens with smoked turkey and ham hocks, and broccoli casserole. That doesn't include all the other food that the others were bringing. The aroma of good food cooking, baking, and boiling could be smelled throughout their large home. Sean Jr. really didn't want to help he just enjoyed watching his father season and cook food. To Sean Jr. it was like an art to mix this with that and make all those wonderful taste and smells.

While Evette waited for her turn in the kitchen, she cleaned the house and combed the girl's hair and made sure they were dressed nicely but she would start her desserts before she got dressed herself. Once in the kitchen should would mix up lemon cake, triple chocolate surprise cake with pecans, sweet potato pies, pecan pies, peach cobbler, 7-Up cakes, and banana pudding.

After Evette has finished making deserts, she makes a blend for fruit smoothies, fruit punch, grape Kool-Aid, and sweet tea. Then she fills the large camping cooler with sodas, Caprisuns, bottled water and an assortment of juice boxes. They are all set for their guest to arrive but of course Henry will be the first to arrive because he has the most important job. Evette wants everything to be perfect because not only do they have all the family coming but Sean also invited everyone from his logging camp and their families. This was going to be a big event.

Sean comes back downstairs in response to the doorbell ringing, it's Henry with two cases of beer in his hands like always. Sean walks with him to the backyard/patio where all the beer and alcohol will be kept in the patio's three built in coolers. Henry fills the grill with charcoal and pre-soaked apple wood and ignites it. He then grabbed beers for Sean and himself, and tossed one of them to Sean with a smile.

"Hey man this is it," smiled Henry "let's do it."

Sean nodded his head, quickly finished his beer, and threw the empty bottle in the trash. "I'll go get the meat," replied Sean as he belched his way back into the house.

"Nigga yo ass aint gonna get drunk and burn up all the damn meat this time are you," sarcastically asked Bruce, seeming to appear from out of no where?

"Fuck you, I'll bet you a rack that you will eat it," responded Henry! "Where in the hell did you come from anyway and where's Michelle and the kids?"

"I still have to go and pick them up from home," said Bruce. "I just stopped by to talk to Sean for a minute. Where is he?"

"He just went inside," said Henry "he was supposed to go and get the rest of the meat." Henry points to the kitchen as he continued to drink his beer and work on the grill. Although there was a lot of space between homes in their neighborhood, the smell of barbecue and down home southern cooking illuminated the upper Anchorage hillside. Then as the morning sun rose over the mountains, family and friends slowly started to trickle in like farmers coming to a harvest celebration. First there was Paul, he was always the first guest to arrive and the last one to leave. Of course he had to bring his new lady-friend, Paul had a new woman for every big family gathering. This time it was Sherri, the time before that it was Jennie, and the fish fry before that it was Stacie. The women in the family often referred to each of his women as being "the flavor of the month".

"Uncle Paul, Uncle Paul," yelled Sean Jr. "Mom, Dad, Uncle Paul is here." Sean Jr. was not surprised to see his uncle with a new lady-friend. He changed women so much even the children expected it.

Next it was Jerome and his wife, Natasha. They have been separated for years but the still showed up to every family function with the kids like a happy family. Natasha seemed to always be tipsy before she stepped a foot out of the car. No one really knows why those two separated but everyone assumed that her heavy drinking had a lot to do with it. And then Sharon pulls into the long driveway with her music blasting and the top let down on her new convertible. Sharon was a big girl but she always liked being flashy. Evon sat in the passenger seat hidden behind her shades as if she had a rough night, followed by Melissa and Monica in another car with the back seat and trunk filled with even more food.

"Hey ladies," said Melissa as she pulls her car right next to Sharon and Evon! "I hope everybody is ready to throw down because we brought a lot of food!"

"Do you ladies need help getting that stuff out of the car," yelled Bruce from the upstairs balcony?

"No we got it," responded Monica "but thanks."

"It's cool, I was on my way down anyway," said Bruce as he disappears from the balcony.

"I'm glad you guys made it," said Evette walking down the stairs case in the middle of the house talking to the other women as they enter the front door with their arms full with food containers! "Yall know where the kitchen is."

"Hey, Hello, What's up girl," they all speak to each other!

"Evon did you invite Jim," asked Evette? Jim was Evon's latest boyfriend that nobody liked because he was white. Jim was actually a pretty nice guy but the family didn't like him because Evon always invited him to her family functions but she wasn't welcome around his family because they hated black people. Or so they thought, but Sean and Evette always had the attitude that Evon was family so her and her guest were always welcome.

Carl and Janet showed up with more beer and alcohol. Janet always brought an Asian dish just to try and impress everyone and they were always delicious. Before the end of the day she would still get upset and be crying about something. Carl was trying to space himself from her so he treated her like shit, but no matter what he did she was always there like his shadow. Carl loved her but he felt smothered by her. They went to the back yard to join everyone else as Sean's employees started to show up with their families as well.

"What's up everybody," said Rico as he walks in the backyard smiling with his date. A slim, petite white lady with bright blue eyes and blonde hair. "Everybody this is Gwen, Gwen this is everybody!" Most of the women in the family ignore him because they view him and his antics as taunting. Rico knows how some of the black women in the family feels about black men dating white women so he always brings a white date just to mess with them. It didn't matter to Rico if it was the men in the family or the women, he was just an authentic shit-starter. Carl just shakes his head and laughs at Rico's antics as he walks past Rico and his date and back into the house.

"What's up brother," Carl said to Sean looking up at him at the top of the stairs? "Evette said you wanted to talk to me."

"I do," responded Sean "go to my room. I'll be

in there in a minute. There's some gunja in my nightstand drawer, why don't you twist us up something." Sean goes down to the kitchen to check on the food where he sees Evette stirring one of the many pots. "What are you doing," screams Sean as he intentionally tries to scare Evette?

"Don't play," she says as she quickly turns around. "You almost got a pot of hot collard greens in your face!"

"Aww baby," smiled Sean.

"Aww baby my ass," replied Evette "don't do that shit! And what do you and my brother have to talk about?"

"Nothing," replied Sean "just some guy talk."

"Mmhhh," shrugged Evette as she rolls her eyes and walks out of the kitchen.

Sean just shook his head as he followed her out of the kitchen. Sean knew that it wasn't over, they had company at the present but he would have to deal with her later when everyone leaves. He just went upstairs with the notion that Evette will be harassing him with "what did Carl do?" later that night. She knows that the only time Sean and her brother (Paul) wants to talk to Carl in private is when some bullshit is going on. Never the less, Sean had to say his piece. When Sean enters his bedroom

Carl is on his cell phone talking and smoking a joint.

"Alright, I'll see you tonight," says Carl as he hangs up the phone and passes the joint to Sean. "So what's up, what did I do now?"

"Who said you did something," replied Sean?

"Come on man, I know how these talks go," said Carl "especially with Paul. You and my brother always busting my balls about something."

"I'm not accusing you of shit, I just wanna talk to you man," said Sean. "Stop being so offensive."

"All I know is yall niggas be tripping over nothing but I always listen. What's wrong to you and Paul aint wrong with me. So you and Paul need to back the fuck up sometimes cuz," responded Carl!

"Look muthafucka, I'm trying to help yo punk ass," replied Sean!

"I'm a grown ass man," inserted Carl!

"I wouldn't give a fuck, don't talk like you beyond getting yo ass kicked," growled Sean!
"Look I know what this is about okay," Carl started to explain. "The truth is I took your cousin on a date one time and that was it, there was no sex involved. We are just friends and nothing else."

"I know it's nothing else because yo bitch ass no what's up right," Sean started to say but he was interrupted by a knock at the bedroom door. In walks Paul.

"Ahh shit, here comes this muthafucka," responded Carl!

"Damn, let me get in the door before you start talking shit about me," said Paul. "What's up Sean? "I know you are not up here trying to talk civilized to this nigga. He don't listen to shit but momma used to always say that a hard head makes a soft ass."

"And who in the hell is going to listen to yo ill planning ass," snapped Carl! "If you keep yo ass out of them damn casinos you might be able to get and keep a descent woman one day. Instead of going around trying to tell somebody else how to treat they woman."

"Man listen, this aint about Paul," inserted Sean.

"I'll be damned if it aint," said Carl. "How this muthafucka gonna talk to anybody with all of the hos he fuck with? And you can't talk either with your head so far up Evette's ass. SEAN!"

"What are you talking about Carl," asked Paul?

"Man this nigga tripping cause he thinks I fucked

his cousin ," insisted Carl.

"Did you," asked Paul?

"This isn't about my cousin or Paul," replied Sean. "Besides Paul can fuck whoever he wants to because he's a bachelor, yo ass aint."

"Sean don't give me that shit like you are the righteous one or some shit," snapped Carl! "You've done dirt too muthafucka or does Evette know how flirty you get after a few drinks. And Paul the only reason they didn't build that new clinic downtown is because you keep the old one in business. I just took her out to dinner, I'm not up to nothing. For the last time get the fuck off my ass please!"

"Don't be worried about what the fuck I be doing," said Paul. "I'm grown youngster, you are the little brother and I'm the big brother so you let that be the last time you get it twisted! Now run tell Momma that shit."

"You need to be focusing on starting your business," inserted Sean. "All this other shit is a waste of time. Me and Evette will not keep bailing you out of failed business plans."
"Fuck that Sean," replied Paul "you aint that nigga's daddy. If he wants to fall then let his ass fall."

"Paul why are you even talking," asked Carl? "I aint never asked yo ass for shit."

"This isn't about money, Paul, or Sean," said Sean referring to himself in the third person. "This is much deeper than that but you seem not to have a clue."

"Janet has a big fucking mouth," replied Carl obviously frustrated at this point. "I knew it. I bet she told Evette about the abortion, that's how yall found out. Damn everybody probably knows now."

"ABORTION," blurted out Paul and Sean simultaneously!

"Ooo, you are just full of tricks," said Paul. "We are all family. Why didn't you or Evette tell me? That's messed up Sean."

"Man I'm too through," said Sean. "I didn't even know anything about no abortion. I've got guest downstairs, I'm tired of wasting my time talking to this dude."

"Why did you bring me up here," asked Carl? "It is you that's wasting my time."

"So if this is not about the abortion, then what is it about," asked Paul?
"That's what I want to know Sean. What the fuck is this shit about," asked Carl?
"Michelle," Sean replied "this is about Michelle."

"Michelle," responded Paul with his mouth and eyes wide open. "Michelle as in Bruce's Michelle?"

Carl didn't say a word, he just stormed out of the room and slammed the door. Paul looked at Sean once again with shock and disbelief apparent on his face. Even though Paul didn't know the entire story just yet, he knew it wasn't good. Sean laid back on his bed and exhaled a sigh of relief. He knows letting Carl's secret out would change their relationship forever but he would no longer have to carry the burden of knowing this secret alone. He just lies there while he contemplates on whether to tell Paul the whole story or not. Sean also realizes that telling Paul would prompt him to make a big scene out of the situation and this was not the day for this.

"Okay, I'm waiting," said Paul.

"Waiting for what," asked Sean with a confused look on his face while rolling another joint? "I know you don't mean you are waiting on this joint. You better wait yo ass down to yo car and get your own shit."

"No man," replied Paul "I'm talking about what's going on with Carl and Michelle?"

"Yeah right, like I'm gone tell yo ass anything," responded Sean.

"That's bullshit Sean," said Paul! "how long have you known about this? When was some body going to tell me? I knew as soon as I went on vacation some shit was going to happen."

"Hold the fuck up," snapped Sean! "I didn't tell your ass nothing because we all know you can't keep shit a secret. Just like in college. And what is this shit about when you go on vacation you knew something would happen like you are the fucking family keeper or some shit? That's what Carl was talking about, we are all grown. You act like you are everybody's damn daddy."

"Look, I'm just trying to guide the family in the right direction because I'm the oldest," replied Paul. "And you should be the most thankful because your head is so far up Evette's ass you need some guidance."

"Look man, you and Carl got me fucked up," said Sean. "Not your sister or any other woman is gonna tell me what to do. Yall muthafuckas are always hating on how me and my wife handle our shit but it's okay when everybody wants me to be the family ATM. Man you know what, you can think and say whatever you want but stop hating. I have a lovely wife, three beautiful kids, my own business, and this big house. My life and marriage is great. Why in the fuck would I take advice from your two week long, relationship having ass?"
"Oh that's cold brother-in-law," laughed Paul.
"What do you want from me? I try."

"I want you to go to your car so we can smoke your shit," replied Sean with laughter of his on as both of them left out of the room and went back downstairs.

THE BETRAYAL

In a crowded boardroom, eleven men sit around a large conference table ending discussions on the month's top agendas. The air so filled with tension that you could taste it. All the men waiting in anticipation for the three law firm partners to return to the room with the verdict. Although there are a few eligible lawyers with the firm. Rico quietly sits there with certainly that he has already made a partner. The others talk and whisper among each other as if they all have an idea that Rico has already been chosen. He's the only black attorney at the firm and everyone believes he is a sure win. They all laugh and tell jokes as Rico thinks about his celebration party with his fellows later tonight. Sean, Bruce, and Henry are going to meet him at home, he'll change clothes and then they'll meet Jerome, Carl and Duane at their favorite bar, or so he thought. All the men sat up in their seats as the partners enter the conference room. Mr. Lynks, the oldest of the three partners, begins to speak as the other two partners stand close by.

"Okay men, I know you all have things to do so I'll make this quick." says Mr. Lynks as he looks around at everybody over his glasses. "This was a hard decision for us to make, you are all a great group of guys and some damn good lawyers, but unfortunately we could only choose one of you. We like to think of each other here at Lynks, Noble, and Greene as family." Mr. Lynks says in a soft tone as Rico smiles from across the table with the certainty of winning. "So without further delay it gives me great pleasure to name Fritz as the new partner."

There is a dead silence in the room for what seemed like forever. Half of the room in shock and the other half in disbelief. Finally the other men start to shake hands and congratulate Fritz on his new job. Rico then jumps up and storms out of the room into his office and slams the door. The other partners head towards the door to see what's going on with Rico, but Mr. Lynks stops them before they can leave the room.

"I'll go talk to him." says Mr. Lynks as he walks out of the conference room and down the hall to Rico's office. He knocks while simultaneously turning the knob to open the door.

"Go away!" yelled Rico.

"What the fuck is your problem son!" inserted Mr. Lynks.

"My problem!" Rico yells and quickly calms down. "My problem is Fritz making partner after all the years of hard work and long hours that I've invested in this firm. Then he makes partner, this is bullshit! If I'm not mistaking, not only is this bullshit, but it could also be perceived as racist."

"Now you slow the fuck down!" shouted Mr. Lynks. "You see, you're right, I smell bullshit all over this building and it seems to be coming from this office!"

"Don't try to switch this shit around." replies Rico. "I earned that partnership just so you could give it to your favorite 'white boy'."

"Look you piece of shit." Mr. Lynks growled. "This isn't about your race or color, this is about me and you."

"Man, what in the hell are you talking about?" asked Rico.

"I'm talking about you working here for years." Mr Lynks responded. "That's your down fall. Ever since you were fresh out of law school you have been working here for years, but at last years company picnic I caught you on your shit. I know the type of women you date and my over-weight daughter is not your type. Unless you thought by dater her was a sure win for partner." Mr. Lynks turns and walks out the door. "By the way, she told me what you did. This is my daughter we are talking about, you're lucky I didn't kick your ass!"

68

"Fuck!" screams Rico as Mr. Lynks closes the door behind himself.

Mr. Lynks sees the other partners in the hallway as he leaves Rico's office.

"What's going on with Rico?" the other two senior partners asked with curiosity and concern.

"Awe, he'll be alright." growled Mr. Lynks while adjusting his tie. "He's lucky he even still has a job." as he continued to walk down the hall to his office.

Meanwhile Rico sits in his office with his head on the desk contemplating on where and when he went wrong. He knew that dealing with the bosses daughter could make things happen for himself, but he also knew it was a very delicate situation. If he played his cards right he could even go as far deceiving her to marry him, which would guarantee him a position in the firm. Though if she ever found out that Rico couldn't stand to be around her and hated her presence, she would be sure to make everything come crumbling down in his face. His plan was working well and fool proof except for one drunken weekend when talking with the homies. Rico left his cellphone on his pocket not knowing Rena heard him telling all his friends how he couldn't stand being around her. He also talked about her weight, pale skin, and figure not knowing that she was listening to everything. Rena cried all weekend from heartache because he really made her feel like she was in love. Though when she consulted her friends about it they all came to the conclusion that she couldn't tell Rico that she heard anything, just go straight to her father with the whole story. So, she did. Rico went into that board meeting on Monday morning totally blind to what had happened. His master plan had been infiltrated and he didn't even have a clue. The longer he sat there and out two and two together, the more he realized he was busted.

"Rico, a Mr. Means is holding for you on line three." a soft-spoken secretary says over the intercom.

Rico quickly answers the call. "What's up Jerome?" asked Rico with despair in his voice.

"Are we still meeting at the usual spot tonight?" Jerome asked. "I heard you've got some good news to tell everybody."

"Yes, I still want to meet everybody, but the good news has changed." says Rico. "But I need a drink all the same."

Back at Sean's house Monica and Melissa argue about about what's wrong with Michelle, not knowing that she has serious relationship problems. They all think it's because of something that Bruce did. Although Bruce does fuck with a lot of women. Michelle if feeling guilty about her own dirt, not considering what Bruce has done in the past. She feels she should tell somebody, but she doesn't have the nerves. Evette has always been there for her and she knows the truth would mean the end of their friendship forever. However She doesn't know that Sharon is aware of everything that is going on. The truth is ever so close to exploding like a time bomb.

"Michelle do you want something to drink?" asked Evette as she gets up from the love seat where two of them were sitting.

"No, I'm fine." answered Michelle. "Thank you anyway."

"Bitch I know you wasn't just asking Michelle because she has created a fucked up life for herself." blurted out Sharon. "This bitch will be alright as long as she..."

"Oh my God." interrupted Melissa while rising up from her seat with nail polish in one hand and the polish brush in the other. "You sound like Evon."

"So what." says Sharon.

"We're suppose to be her fiends Sharon." replies Monica. "Right now she needs our support, not put downs and talking

shit."

"Monica is right, Sharon." inserted Melissa. "Michelle is the victim here. I mean we all love Evon, but the shit she is doing is wrong."

"Bullshit!" replied Sharon. "She's not all innocent in this situation, so you and Monica need to shut the fuck up! Victim, what victim? Bitch please!."

"Okay Sharon, that's enough." says Evette as she sets back on the love seat with tissue to wipe Michelle's eyes and comfort her. "Melissa's right, you shouldn't be trying to upset her even more, we are her friends. Sharon please understand that she needs all of us right now. You talking shit to her isn't going to help her any."

"Come on Sharon." says Monica. "Right is right. Michelle does need our support right now."

"Why are you talking to me like that?" cries Michelle finally breaking her silence as she wipes the tears from her face. "I was there for you when you went through your divorce with Charles. I didn't talk shit to you or try to make you feel worse, so why are you doing it to me?" as she sobs.

"She's got a point Sharon." said Evette.

"Hold on." responded Sharon. "You were there for me, I'll give you that and I am grateful that all of you were there for me, but I'm pissed off because it's all about friendship and all of you are judging Evon and she's not here to defend herself. Y'all talk about friendship, but where is your loyalty to her? Is she not our sister also?"

"She knew we were all going to be here today." says Melissa. "If there's nothing going on then why isn't she here?"

"Because she knows she is in the wrong and she betrayed

me." says Michelle crying heavy on the love seat while Evette comforts her.

"Look I can't take no more of this shit." snarled Sharon as she jumps up out of her seat. "I'm going to go spend some time with Evon before she leaves for Seattle. Y'all should come with me; we are all losing a close friend. This bitch can stay here and bathe in her own wickedness."

"Hold on Sharon." Evette says, jumping out of her seat and grabbing Sharon by the arm. Melissa and Monica watch with their mouths open in suspense, and shock. "I'm sorry Sharon for grabbing your arm like that, but I don't want you to leave yet."

"Why?" asked Sharon. "Y'all wanna pass judgment on me too without hearing what I got to say."

"No." Evette said in a low whisper. "It took me a long time to catch on, but I can't tell you know something we don't."

"What are you talking about Evette?" asked Sharon as she sits back down.

"Evette is right, Sharon spit it out." replied Monica.

"Yeah I want to know what you got to say in defense of your precious Evon." says Michelle. "Just remember it's not your husband she's fucking!
"Enough of this shit!" shouts Sharon throwing her purse on the couch. "I talked with Evon that day we were playing spades and she is not secretly seeing Bruce. Bruce has been meeting Evon to ask her information about Michelle. Poor Evon's only mistake is letting Bruce get her in the middle of that shit. I'm pissed off because she's trying to turn us all against Evon. The truth be told, Evon is probably the only thing that's keeping Bruce from better her nasty ass."

"Fuck you, okay Sharon! Fuck you!" cried Michelle.

"Fuck you too nasty bitch." responded Sharon taking off her earing and kicking her shoes.

"That's enough!" yelled Evette. "Y'all are not gonna tear up my house."

"What's your problem with me?" asked Michelle with tears in her eyes. "Evon is seeing my husband and you're mad at me, I don't get it."

"Bruce told Evon everything." replied Sharon. "And you're making her look bad when she's not around to defend herself, but that's okay because every dog has her day."

"Whatever Sharon, whatever." said Michelle. "Just because you can't keep a man doesn't mean you can hate on everybody else."

"Whatever?" Sharon replied with disbelief. "For your information, Bruce told Evon everything. He knows you've been fucking Carl, you stupid bitch." Sharon walks out and leaves everybody in disbelief of what they just heard. Melissa and Monica now feeling betrayed by Michelle because they actually believed that Evon would cross their friendship like that. Evette also feeling betrayed because all this time she welcomed Michelle into her home and tried to comfort her just to find out she brought all this on herself. Michelle was shocked more than anyone. Her secret was out and her husband was not having an affair, but he knew about hers. Evette was her best friend and she knew how she felt about her friends dating her little brother. The mistrust she bestowed in her friend was almost irreversible and the pain of everybody knowing her shameful secret was ripping through her heart like a knife the very instance the truth was revealed. The worst of it was the fact that she betrayed her best friend.

A TEST OF FRIENDSHIP

Bruce and Sean sit at a crowded smoke filled bar waiting for the rest of their homies to show up. The two men haven't spoke on the Carl and Michelle situation the entire time they have been sitting there. Though they both know it has to be addressed sooner or later. After all, they are friends, like family and all this secrecy, private meetings and back stabbing has to stop. But that's what makes them such a close family, the drama. Oh yeah, drama, the number one ingredient in a strong family recipe. Everybody has an uncle, cousin, or aunt that smokes crack or some shit, but they're still family.

"Where the fuck is everybody?" asked Bruce as he clicks snifters with Sean. "They should have been here half an hour ago."
"Yeah what's up with that?" replied Sean. "Rico is the one who wanted to meet here and his ass ain't even here." At that time in walks Paul, Jerome, and Henry. All three men dressed up looking good and smelling clean, ready for a night on the town.

"Where is Rico?" Paul asked as he approaches the bar.

"What's up fellas?" replied Sean. "I don't know, but I've been calling him and he's not answering his cell phone."

"Well, I did talk to him at his office earlier today." said Jerome. "But he didn't sound happy."

"Oh shit." responded Paul. "I hope everything went okay because he was all psyched about making partners at his firm."

"How can he not make partner with the bosses daughter sucking his dick?" replied Henry.

About that time Rico walks in with Carl and Duane. "Hey what's up everybody?" says Rico as he pulls up a bar stool to join his friends. "I might as well get it out in the open now, so that everybody can hear it from me. Mr. Lynks found out I was just fucking with his daughter to secure my position as partner, so of course I didn't get the position."

"Are you serious?" asked Bruce.

"That's bullshit." replied Carl.

"How in the hell did he find out what your intentions were?" asked Duane.

"She told him herself." replied Rico.

"But how did she know what you were up to?" asked Sean. "The last time I seen her at your pad she seemed to be wrapped around your finger."

"That's the fuck up part of it all." says Rico. "Remember last week when I was telling you and Bruce about how I only deal with her cause I'm on a mission. In reality I really can't stand to be in that fat bitch's presence or even to hold a normal conversation with her ass. And remember I said that she can't fuck, but it was worth it cause she had some cold head. Well, come to find out when I went to work, my cell phone was on in my pocket and she heard the whole conversation. So, naturally I didn't get the job."

"Now that's a reason to drink." said Carl. "That's why Janet is about to be out the door. I can't take this, being in a relationship anymore. I can't have a life of my own, she's always nagging me about shit."

"Nigga, Janet ain't changed. She's been like that ever since y'all have met." said Duane. "You just want to fuck other bitches."

"I keep telling that nigga to let them hood rats go." laughed Paul.

"Carl's just talking shit, he ain't leaving Janet." said Sean.

"Man you got me fucked up." replied Carl. "I got hoes all over Anchorage, not including my rats I got on Elmendorf."

"Oh yeah." says Bruce. "It ain't nothing wrong with that. Nigga when I was young I was fucking a lot of bitches too. I even fucked a couple of niggas wives. Know what I'm saying Carl."

Carl didn't say anything, he just quickly took another drink of cognac.

"My little brother is just talking shit." said Paul. "He ain't fucking nobody but Janet." says Paul trying his best to defuse the situation before it escalates.

"That's where you got me fucked up." replies Carl. "I'm not your little brother, I'm a grown ass man."

"Man chill the fuck out." snapped Sean with no concern to get into the conversation.

"No Sean, let this young brother talk." says Bruce. "So you have let a married woman suck your dick, huh?"

"All I'm saying is that if a muthafucka can't control his bitch he should keep her on a leash instead of going out fucking other bitches himself." Carl replied. "Of course you know what I'm saying, huh Bruce."

"No, actually I don't." says Bruce. "Because all the married women I ever messed with in my life was a completely different scenario"

"Bullshit." said Carl. "Somebodies wife is somebodies wife no matter how you try to put it."

"Carl is right, I've fucked plenty of married white chicks." laughed Rico not knowing the seriousness of the conversation.

"And they all wanted it, I didn't rape nobody. Shit man, Bruce, when Michelle went to Kingston with Evette, me and you picked up two married Broads together."

"That was different." responded Bruce.

"How in the fuck is that shit different?" asked Carl.

"Yeah Bruce, how is that different?" asked Rico.

"Because they were strangers." replied Bruce. "They were not any of my homies wives."

At that moment Bruce and Carl quickly jumped up from their bar stool and everybody got an instant reality check on what this whole conversation was about. Bruce grabs Carl by the shirt and throws him across a nearby table. Immediately Sean and Paul grab Bruce while Duane and Rico try to restrain Carl. Then out of no where Sharon walks in.

"Everybody calm the fuck down!" yelled Paul.

"Hold the fuck up." shouted Duane. "You mean to tell me that all this is about you fucking Michelle. Carl we have been friends since the third grade. I know you're not fucking Michelle, nigga are you crazy."

"Nigga fuck you!" yells Carl.

"Fuck me!" Duane replies as he releases the grip on Carl's arm. "Paul and Sean should let Bruce go, you deserve to get your ass kicked."

"Are all you muthafuckas crazy!" asked Sharon as she steps in the middle of everybody. There was an instant silence. "Bruce you need to calm down, you're not completely innocent in this situation. Carl me and you need to talk right now, outside." as Carl storms out towards the front door. "And for you Mr. Bruce, I know that shit..."

"Sharon stay out of this." interrupted Paul. "This is between men folk."

"Nigga ain't nobody asked you shit." growled Sharon. "You ain't nobodies damn daddy. You need to keep track of your own drama queens and wicked ways. Besides Michelle really is my friends, so that makes it have something to do with me." as she turned her attention back on Bruce. "Mr. Bruce, like I was saying, I know that shit Carl did was fowl, but this shit is deeper that Carl. Then you got Evon all mixed up in this shit. It's fucked up it had to be Carl, I don't know what he was thinking, but with all the creeping you do, don't you realize this shit was bound to happen."

"So what are you saying Sharon?" asked Bruce. "It's my fault my wife is fucking my best friends little brother."

"No, all I'm saying is that karma is a muthafucka ain't it." Sharon softly says as she turns and walks out.

TIME TO REPENT

The next day Sean and Paul sit out on the balcony of Sean's master bedroom drinking coffee trying to make sense of what happened the night before. Although they both seem to be unsurprised about Bruce's actions. Paul seems to be really disappointed and upset. Pacing back and forth smoking cigarettes one after another. Keeping in mind that Evette just got a phone call downstairs and they are almost certain that it is Sharon filling her in on everything that happened the night before.

"Why isn't Carl or Bruce answering their cell phones? Asked Paul constantly hanging up the phone and pushing the redial button again.

"I don't know!" replied Sean.

"Why is Evette on the phone so long?" asked Paul.

"I don't know!" Sean replied again.

"If Carl is fucking Michelle nobody knows how long it's been going on." Paul stated. "So does all those kids belong to Bruce? And What does he plan to do when Janet finds out what's going on. Ah man, and not to mention that when my mom finds out, she's going to be pissed."

"Nigga, will you calm the fuck down, damn!" shouted Sean. "I can't think with all your bitching and moaning. Here, roll us a joint and give me that phone." said Sean passing Paul the box of weed and snatching the phone from his hand.

"Man if Momma asked me about anything, I'm just going to play dumb." says Paul.

"What I can't understand is why didn't Carl tell one of us." Sean pondered. "There has got to be a reasonable explanation.

And for a man finding out someone was fucking his wife, Bruce didn't seem to be that pissed off."

"Bruce didn't seem all that pissed because he's been dealing with this for some time now." replied Paul.

"Naw man, it's something more than that." Sean responded. "Bruce and Michelle have been having marital problems for a couple of years now. She has been trying to get up the nerves to leave Bruce for a long time. Bruce has some broad up in Fairbanks he's been seeing for a long time, but what I can't understand is how does Carl get mixed up in all of this."

The two men sat there smoking joints and drinking beer trying to come up with a reasonable explanation to all this madness and confusion. They both know that the only way to salvage their brother's reputation and their friendship with Bruce is to get to the bottom of this fiasco. But there are too many loose ends, too many unanswered questions. It's now noon the next day and nobody has heard from Bruce or Carl. Just as soon as they come up with a possible scenario, the facts just don't add up. Now at a loss of words, time is working against them because they both know that when Evette gets off the phone, she will be looking at them for an explanation.
"What in the hell happened at the bar last night?" angrily asked Evette as she busts in the room and slams the door behind her.

"Hey baby." replied Sean.

"Don't hey baby me!" Evette responded.

"What's up sis?" says Paul.

"Sean why didn't you tell Carl that Bruce was on to him before he showed up last night?" asked Evette. "What if Bruce would have lost it and shot him or something. You know that there is such a thing as a crime of passion."

"Bruce wouldn't do anything like that." responded Paul. "He was just blowing off steam."

"Paul shit the fuck up." blurted out Evette. "You should know more about crimes of passion that anybody. If that girl you dated last year sliced your tires after you didn't call her for four days, what do you think a man would do if he found out his friend has been fucking his wife of thirteen years. Can anybody tell me why Bruce and Carl aren't answering their house phones or cell phones? If anything happens to my brother the two of you......" Evette stops in mid sentence as the doorbell interrupts her.

"Baby don't worry, we will find them." says Sean.

"Yeah Evette, calm down." says Paul.

"Fuck you Paul, don't tell me to calm down." yelled Evette. "Momma don't know about this...yet! But she will find out. All your efforts and everything you did to help your little brother. And for you Mr. Sean." Evette calmly says, "Bruce is your best friend and I know you knew something was going on for quite some time. You better find them. Now if you gentlemen will excuse me, I have to answer my front door."

As Evette turns and walks out of the room with obvious anger, Sean and Paul just shook their heads in frustration. They knew that Evette was really worried about Carl and even more upset that Sean and Paul were sitting in the bedroom smoking joints and not out looking for them. Then when the two men thought that matters couldn't get any worse, Evette opens the door to find Michelle and Janet standing there. "We need to talk to you." both women said simultaneously. Sceptically Evette lets them in.

"I know what's going on now Evette." sobs Michelle. "I am so sorry, please forgive me."

"Where's my brother?" asked Evette.

"I don't know where he's at." responded Janet. "But I know what he's up to."

At that time Sean and Paul came walking down the stairs both in shock. Of course they both have to know what's going on, so why were they there and why are they not in a cat-fight by now? As the two men descend down the stairs they can only wonder what is going on with Michelle and Janet showing up at the front door together the day after both their husbands were fighting in the club the night before.

"Well, well come on down fellows." Evette replied. "This is something y'all need to hear."

"What are you talking about Evette? Is Carl okay?" asked Paul.

"He's alright, but apparently these ladies know more about what's going on than my husband and brother." Evette replies.

"What do you ladies know?" asked Sean immediately turning his attention to Michelle and Janet.

"Well it started last night." Janet explained as she starts to cry. "Carl came home from the club like any other night smelling like a brewery and horny. But of course I was mad because he had gone out all night, so I didn't want him climbing his drunk ass on top of me. So when he realizes he ain't getting no pussy he blows up. Started calling me all kind of Asian bitches, fried rice hoe and shit like that. Started saying how he was tired of me anyway. WAS! I mean he's saying 'was' like it's over. So I asked him what is he trying to say, but he just threw up his hands and walked away." Evette passed her a tissue; Janet wiped her eyes, blew her nose and continued. "then about an hour goes by and I'm upstairs crying like an idiot when I hear a car pull in the driveway. So I go out to the garage to see who it is. I slowly cracked the door going into the garage, just so I can peek in. Not getting in his business or anything like that, but I want to know who's coming to my house this late at night. I then see Carl and Bruce talking. The both of them are

84

apparently drink, so they're talking real loud."

"And at the time you don't know what's going on, so you think it's just Bruce." inserted Paul.

"Right." said Janet. "But I listened to their conversation anyway."

"What did you hear?" asked Sean with a serious concern.

"Apparently, Bruce was going to open an new night club in Fairbanks and a roofing company here in Anchorage, both worth a lot of money. There's also another woman and child in Fairbanks, but he knows if he leaves Michelle, under Alaska law he would have to give Michelle half of everything. Though if he could prove that Michelle was unfaithful, he could divorce her with nothing. So, he paid Carl ten thousand dollars to have an affair with Michelle. I heard Carl tell Bruce the same thing he said to me. That it worked out perfect for him cause he was tired of my ass anyway and he knew that when I find out what was going on I would leave anyway. Then they laughed and talked for a while longer then Carl got in the car with Bruce then they left."

"Sean, if you knew about this I'll never forgive you!" growled Evette.

"I didn't know nothing." replied Sean. "They played me just like everybody else."

"Fuck that!" yelled Evette. "You and Paul better hope y'all find them before we do. Come on girls, y'all can ride with me."

"well, I'll be a muthafucka." says Paul as he turns and looks at Sean.

"Fuck!" replied Sean as he grabbed his keys and both men headed out the door.

In the mean time across town Melissa and Monica are at a day spa getting their hair, nails and facials done. It's like a weekly routine for these ladies, same place, same time. Though for some reason today it was different because no one else showed up. Even thought no one else showed up, these two fashion divas wouldn't dream of missing their day spa appointment.

"Hey Melissa." says Monica finally breaking the silence. "Don't you think it's kind of strange that nobody else showed up or called."

"Yeah, you're right." responded Melissa. "It's not like them to not call, but Evon has been acting funny lately. Sharon was suppose to pick her up Evette, but her fat ass probably had to stop for a catfish plate or something!" as the both of them start laughing and speaking in their native tongue. Melissa and Monica give each other that look as if they were both thinking 'we can crack jokes on Sharon, she is our friend, but I know these bitches didn't! But before anybody could check them about it they're interrupted by Monica's cell phone ringing.

"Hello." says Monica after a couple of rings. "This is she. Yes. What! Say What! That's bullshit! I know where they live. I'm on my way."

What was that all about?" asked Melissa.

"Girl we've got to go." replied Monica. "That was Evon's sister, she said Evon is over at Jim's family's house upset and crying. She thinks his mom might of hit her."

"Bullshit!" replied Melissa. "Where is my purse?" as they both rushed out the door right in the middle of their manicure. On the way to Jim's house Melissa immediately called up Rico and Jerome for back up just in case things are a lot worse than they think.

"Did you talk to Sharon or Evette?" asked Monica.

"No, I tried, but neither one of them are answering their cell phones." Melissa replied. "But Rico represented Jim's brother once, so he knows where they live. Him and Jerome are on the way."

As they pull up in front of their house everyone is in the front yard yelling and screaming. They could tell that Jim and Evon were defending each other, but they were overwhelmingly out numbered. Jim's family knew that with the arrival of Evon's friends matters would only escalate. And like a clock-work Rico's Mercedes pulled in right behind Monica's car. Jim's brother, Chris, sees Rico and immediately walks over to his car to try and calm things down.

"Oh thank goodness." replied Chris walking towards Rico. "You're a lawyer, maybe you can calm down this situation."

"Man fuck that lawyer shit!" yelled Rico. "Evon is my family, so I'd suggest you back the fuck up white boy!"

"What are you talking about?" asked Chris. "This isn't a black or white thing, it's about two..."

"Bullshit cracker!" interrupted Jerome.

"Hey now, calm down." responded Jim's uncle Scott. "There's no need for name calling there young feller."

"Come on, let's go Evon!" demanded Melissa.

"No, y'all don't understand." cried Evon.

"Girl don't be stupid." says Monica. "I know you like white boys, but it's obvious Jim comes from a family of nigger haters. There are other out there, he ain't the one."

"She's right Evon." responded Rico. "They are never going to approve of their son or nephew dating a black woman."

87

"Now you just hold up right there." replied Jim's mother finally breaking her silence walking down from the porch. "Is that what this hostility is all about? You think I disapprove of their relationship because she is black. Well that's really sad that you all feel that way, but it is obvious she hasn't been telling you the truth. I only disapprove of this relationship because I disapprove of my own child. This family knows Jim as Jill, my first born daughter. This ain't about black or white you idiot!" as she turns and walks back into the house.

Melissa, Monica, Jerome, and Rico all turned and looked at each other in shocking disbelief. Silence came over everyone as if they had been muted with a remote control. They had all been friends for years and no one had a clue that Evon was gay. Overwhelmed with shame and embarrassment, Evon runs to her car in tears and drives off.

"Evon, wait!" yelled out Monica. Then she and Melissa get in their car and speed off after her.

"We really apologize to you folks." explained Rico with an urgency to defuse this whole situation. "Evon is out family. We thought she was in a racial situation, we didn't know that version of the story. Once again we apologize for any inconvenience." Looking at Jerome for him to agree.

"Man, fuck that!" replied Jerome. "Don't be trying to talk professional now. Nigga yo ass ain't in court now."

"Let's go." said Rico. "Let's just go." as they get in the car and drive off.

A TWISTED
TRIANGLE

It has been a week since anyone has seen or heard from Bruce or Carl. This whole fiasco has the family torn. Half of the family feels upset and confused for trying to make sense of it all. The other half of the family feels anger and betrayal, but they all have one mutual concern. Where are they? But there were too many unanswered questions. How could they plan such a scheme without any of the fellows knowing about their plot? Sean and Bruce were best friends and business partners. How could Sean not know anything? And why were Evette and Sharon the only ones interested in getting to the bottom of this? And since that day, in the Schultz from yard, no family member that was present hasn't said anything to the rest of the family about Evon and Jim, Jill. Really I was too many questions and not enough answers.

Duane and Henry sit at a bar in downtown Anchorage taking shots of Cabo Wabo and chasing it with Alaskan Amber. They were both on a business trip in Chicago, so neither of them knows anything about what's been going on. As the two men sit and continue to drink, Duane's cell phone rings. He looks at the caller ID and sees that it's Carl, so he answers.

"What's up?" asked Duane as he throws back another shot. "Come and have some drinks with us. We're downtown sitting at the bar."

"Nah, I can't right now." responded Carl. "Who's all with you anyway?"

"Just me and Henry, we just got back from Chicago." said Duane. "I haven't seen anyone since we got back. No body wanted to answer his or her phones, so we came by ourselves. You know fuck it."

"Right, right." quickly responded Carl. "I'll let you get back to do you player. I was just wondering if you had talked to my sister or Sean. That's all, I'll call you later."

Both men hand up their cell phones and momentarily sink into deep thought. Carl wondering if any of the family members was on to them. If so, did Duane know. Duane tries to figure out why would Carl call his phone looking for Sean or Evette. At that second all his thoughts were interrupted when a sexy black women sat next to him. Perfectly curved, dark-golden skin, smooth and flawless with the scent of expensive perfume.

"Damn!" Henry replied softly, referring to the family that just sat at the bar.

"I'm on it!" quickly inserted Duane as he throws back another shot and turns around to introduce himself. But as they make eye contact his attitude instantly changes. "It's you!" he replied with the look on his face as if he had seen a ghost.

"What's up Duane?" she asked. "How have you been doing?"

"I'm good, okay I guess, I mean I haven't been dumped lately." Duane sarcastically replies.

"Wait a minute. You two know each other?" asked Henry.

"Yeah, remember about a year ago when I said I was starting to get serious with somebody?" says Duane. "Then she just up and disappeared."

"Yeah, I remember that." acknowledged Henry.

"This is Rhonda." says Duane. "Rhonda this is my good friends Henry."

"Nice to meet you Henry." said Rhonda. "And I didn't dump you, my National Guard unit got activated and I was sent to

Iraq."

"Sure, right." said Duane. "You just forgot to call."

"Bullshit." Rhonda said frowning. "I called you a hundred times from Iraq, you never accepted my calls."

"That was you?" asked Duane. As they both stare into each other's eyes, the past instantly forgiven as they burst into laughter and hug each other. They continue to laugh and talk late into the evening. Until their unexpected reunion was interrupted by an unfortunate event.

"Excuse me Duane." Rhonda said. "I have to go to the ladies room." as she turns to get off the bar stool, she looses her prosthetic leg like a drunk dropping a beer on the sidewalk. "Are you okay?" Duane asked in total shock.

"Yeah, I'm fine." replied Rhonda as she frantically tries to re-attach her prosthetic leg with water eyes. "I stepped on a land mine outside of Karbala then woke up a week later in a military hospital minus one leg. But I understand that I'm not your type or any mans type anymore."

"Don't say shit like that." says Duane as he grabs her in his arms and pulls her closer to him feeling her soft breasts press up against his chest. 'Damn she feels and smells so good' he thought to himself. "You are just as jazzy and gorgeous as you were the last time I saw you. Come on, let's get out of here."

"Okay." she responded with a smile on her face as if that was the first time she had a reason to smile in a long time. "But what about your friend?" asked Rhonda. "He'll be alright." said Duane looking at Henry over at the pool tables as they walk out of the door. Henry sees them leaving out of the corner of his eye and smiles. Everything is automatically understood, almost like an animal instinct.

Across town, Melissa, Evette, and Monica think deeply in

91

silence on the were about of Carl and Bruce. Where could they be? And why haven't they tried to contact anyone by now? Maybe there's something wrong or were they looking in the wrong places. Maybe they are not even in Anchorage anymore. Did they leave town? But why? And all at once unexpectedly Melissa breaks the silence with an excellent idea. Or so she thought.

"Hey guys." said Melissa. "Remember Duane and Henry went to Chicago. I bet they are hanging out at Duane's place. Nobody has looked for them there."

"Let's go!" blurted out Evette.

On the way to Duane's place Evette notices that Melissa doesn't feel well. She almost looks as if she could pass out any minute. Which is kind of strange because Melissa is always in the gym and eating right. She is a health nut junky.

"Girl are you okay?" asked Evette.

"Yeah, I'm fine. I think it was something I ate." Melissa answered.

"Okay, we're here." says Monica as she pulls her car into Duane's driveway.

"I don't see any of their cars." Evette said as they get out of the car.

"That's cool, I have a key." replied Melissa fumbling through her purse as they approached the front door. Evette and Monica both look at each other in shock and confusion. Both women wondering why Melissa has a key to Duane's house. But as soon as the door opens there is Rhonda spread wide open on the couch moaning loudly. It was quite obvious that she was really enjoying her reunion with Duane because no one hear the door open. Everyone knows sex on the couch means coming in the door and passionately going at it. The scent of sex was in the air and there was Duane on top of her trying to drill her with every inch and centimeter he had to offer. He was forcing himself inside her so deep and intense, she was caught up in uncontrollable orgasms and moaning so loud that no one could hear anything else. Unexpectedly Melissa drops her keys on the floor and immediately loses it.

"Duane, what the fuck do you think you're doing!" yelled Melissa

"What the hell is this shit!" Duane yells back jumping up to reach for his pants.

"Well Melissa." says Monica. "It's obvious we caught him at a bad time. And neither Bruce or Carl appear to be here, so let's go."

"Wait baby, you don't understand. Let me explain." pleaded Duane as he chased Melissa out the door.

"Melissa stop!" demanded Duane. "Will you talk to me?"

"TALK, nigga fuck you, talk about what!" growled Melissa. "How you was fucking some one legged bitch on your couch when you were suppose to be on a business trip in Chicago. Or how it's about time we let everybody know how we feel about each other. Oh, let me guess, you don't remember saying all that shit to me."

"It's not like that." pleaded Duane. "I didn't think anybody knew I was back in town!"

"Oh, that's real fucking classy." replied Melissa. "And to think I was waiting for you to get back from Chicago to tell you I was pregnant, but there's no for you to concern yourself with that because I'm not having it!"

She jumps into the driver's seat of Monica's car and slams the door with Duane knocking on the window begging her

93

to open the door. Evette and Monica just sit there in silence as she puts the car in gear and pulls off. Melissa only makes it about a half block from Duane's house and the bursts into tears.

NO ROOM TO RECONCILE

Evon sits on the edge of her bed crying as she packs her bags for her trip to Seattle. She is deeply torn between the decision to stay with her family and friends in Alaska or to pursue her career out of state. She knows if she leaves state everyone will be sad because no one wants to see her leave. Though this job offer in Seattle may be the only chance for her to further her career. She was torn between career and family. As she sobs on the side of her bed contemplating, there was a knock at the door.

"Who is it?" sobbed Evon.
"It's me." replied Jill from the other side of the door.

"Open the door, we need to talk. Please!" said Jill.

"I'm coming." said Evon as she walks towards the door and opens it. "Come in Jill."

"Are you sure it's okay?" replied Jill. "I don't think nobody followed me here or do you think I should disguise myself to come see you."

"Jill this is not the time to start some shit." responded Evon. "I'm not in the mood."

"Are you fucking crazy?" growled Jill. "Bitch the shit started when you had Rico and the gang show up at my mother's house trying to fight my family because of your lies. Remember for the last year you were suppose to tell everybody the truth about us. Or maybe the shit started when it slipped your mind to tell me you were moving to Seattle."

"Can we please not talk about this right now." says Evon. "I have a heavy load on my heart and mind, can you please just give it a rest."

"You don't ever have to worry about talking to me anymore." replied Jill. "You don't have to hide me from your friends anymore and you don't have to keep your sexuality a secret anymore because everybody knows. You get to run away to Seattle and start a whole new life without me. So have a nice new life in Seattle and fuck you!" as she turns and walks out slamming the door on her way out.

Evon sat on the edge of her bed crying and thinking about how could she face everybody again after her secret was out. Also, everyone knows she was helping Bruce in his wicked scam. But the truth of the matter was that she was in the blind about the whole thing. Nor did she have any idea that Bruce and Carl were in cahoots together. Evon genuinely thought she was helping out a friend, not assisting Bruce in some crazy divorce scam. Why did she choose her? And not only did she feel none of her friends would trust her again, but they also think she was helping Bruce. Now she's worried about what they think since she had kept her gay life a secret. She knows that most straight women think if you're gay that you want them. It doesn't matter if they're your type or not. "This job in Seattle couldn't have came at a better time." she thought. When she was interrupted by a knock on the front door. At first she hesitates to pull herself together and wipe the tears from her eyes. She walks over to the door just knowing that it is Jill coming back to argue some more. She then opens the door and CRACK! Right in the face.

"Bitch you think I'm gonna let you leave that easy!" screams Michelle as she watches Evon fall backwards onto the floor.

"What the fuck is your problem Michelle!" yelled Evon quickly jumping up and grabbing a lamp ans swinging for Michelle's head, but misses. "Are you fucking crazy?"

"I came to get some answers!" yelled Michelle. "Like does Bruce and Carl plan to cut you in on the money? Or is it just a coincidence that you plan to move to Seattle at the same time Bruce and Carl pull their disappearing act? Are they waiting on you in Seattle? Is that where they're at?"

'You're really stupid." replied Evon. "I didn't have nothing to do with that shit, he just asked me to help him because he thought you were cheating. Any deals he had with Carl was without me knowing."

"Bitch you ruined my marriage." says Michelle. "Can't you at least tell me the truth now." as she starts to cry in despair because in her mind she believes Evon knows everything that's going on with Bruce.

"You got a lot of fucking nerves coming in here pointing fingers at somebody!" bluntly responded Evon. "How dare you accuse me of lying! I told you I don't know anything about no plan as far as your marriage, let's not forget that you were really fucking Carl. I had nothing to do with that, but I'm sure if you think about it long enough you'll realize what ruined your marriage. So get the fuck out of my house."

Evon sat on her couch crying think about how messed up her situation was. She thought about leaving Anchorage and all her friends and family behind. They were all she had and to leave her family meant leaving everything. Missing out on all the family gatherings and holidays. The kid's birthdays, partying with her home girls, or just having loved ones around. They'd all be gone. Then again Seattle is only a two hour flight away. Although deep in her heart she knew that she and Michelle had been friends since high school and that she should go try to salvage her friendship. What about Jill though. She really did love her, but coming out of the closet was a lot harder than she thought especially when the people closest to her didn't have a clue. She really didn't want to leave, but a new job offer out of town was a perfect get away. Evon thought deep and hard for hours about what was the right thing to do. Then after a long deliberation with her inner self struggling with what was really in her heart, she went into her bedroom. She walked out shortly after with her things and headed to the airport.

Back across town Duane pulls into Melissa's driveway and

puts his car in park. He doesn't get out right away; instead he just sits there and tries to collect his thoughts. He feels that he really loves Melissa, but he also was still in love with Rhonda. His relationship with Melissa blossomed over night shrouded in secrecy from everyone around them. How could he keep it a secret or was it ever meant to be a secret. After all he thought that Melissa truly loved him and she wanted to tell everybody the whole time they had been seeing each other. Though after all, it was Duane who wanted to wait. Maybe it was because he knew their relationship was not meant to be. What to do now that she's pregnant? Rhonda was just as gorgeous as Melissa, but with one leg he knew that in a sense he would always have to take care of her. But still she was so incredibly stunning with her one leg, fucking bush. He went through all this over and over in his mind all the way to Melissa's house. Now he was just sitting in her driveway thinking. Melissa was pregnant and Rhonda was expecting to pick up where they left off. What to do, what to do?

"Duane, why did you give her a key." Duane whispered to himself. You could have kept fucking both of them. Fuck it, I have to fix this shit. Do the right thing man!" He took a deep breath and rings the doorbell. There was about a ten second pause, he then rings the doorbell again.

"Who is it?" asked Melissa from the inside of the door.

"It's me." replied Duane. "Please open the door, I want to talk to you."

"Talk about what?" Melissa says as she swiftly opens the door.

"Hey listen, I don't want to upset you more than I already have." says Duane. "I just want to talk to you."

"Come on in." she says as she steps aside to let him enter the house.

"Thank you." Duane replies as he closes the door behind

himself. "Are you okay? How are you doing?"

"Talk!" Melissa promptly replies.

"Yeah, umm, I just wanted to tell you." Duane started to say. "That it wasn't what it looked like. Remember I told you about Rhonda and how serious things were getting between us. But then everything just went bad."

"Yeah, then she dumped you." inserted Melissa.

"And you were there for me." replied Duane. "And I love you for that, but she didn't dump me I went out of town on business and I came back. She had been sent to Iraq with her National Guard unit, I didn't even know she was in the Guard. Then when I saw that she had lost her leg I really felt bad because I never answered her calls. Then after several drinks it kind of just happened. I really love you and I want to take care of you and our child. So please forgive me, she means nothing to me. I love you."

"Nigga get the fuck out of my house." Melissa calmly replied as she swiftly re-opens the door to him to leave. "Bye."

Duane didn't respond, he just walked out the door.

WHAT'S REALLY GOING ON

Michelle was waiting on Sharon's ex-husband to get to Anchorage from Dallas. Sharon told her that he was coming to visit his son for a couple of weeks and Michelle hoped that she could get him to help her out or at least shed a little more light on things. He owns a private investigation firm in Dallas and it was rumored that he was the best. People used his professional services all over the United States with reliable results. If anybody could get to the bottom of all this, Jasper Shaw would. Michelle and Sharon sit outside of the Delta terminals at the airport waiting on Jasper's flight to arrive. Sharon didn't fill him in on what was going on so Michelle was hoping that he would look in to it as a friend, but he wasn't sure that he would even look into it. As they sat there talking among themselves, his flight started to unboard. Then all of a sudden Sharon got quiet as she noticed her ex-husband walking though the terminal. Jasper was a tall dark-skinned man with a bulky, but muscular build. He was clean shaved as always with strong defined facial features. Sharon momentarily got excited as soon as she laid eyes on him and walked over to give him a hug. He was looking good.

"Hey!" said Sharon as she reaches up to hug Jasper. "How was your flight?"

"It was just fine." replied Jasper in a deep voice. "And how have you been?"

"Everything is just fine with me." said Sharon releasing her grip from around his neck and turning to look at Michelle.

"And how are you doing Michelle?" asked Jasper as he leans over to give Michelle a hug. "Long time no see."

"I'm not doing so well." answered Michelle a she starts to

explain what had happened while they walked downstairs to the baggage claim.

"That sounds real fishy." responded Jasper after Michelle and Sharon finished feeling him in on everything that had been going on. "Well I am on vacation and want to spend time with my son, but during the day when he is at school I will do what I can."

"Thank you." Michelle said as they walked to the car.

"Hello." Sharon said answering her cell phone. "Yeah, we got him. I'll stop by there before Jas gets out of school. That was Evette nem'. They want to see you, so I told her we would stop by there. I hope you don't mind."

"No, that's fine." said Jasper. "I want to see everybody anyway."

"Sean!" yells Evette. "Are you upstairs?"

"Yeah, I'm in our room." responded Sean. "What's up?"

"I just wanted to let you know that Sharon picked Jasper up at the airport and they're on their way over to our house." said Evette running up the stairs. When she made it up the stairs and into the room she caught Sean getting out of the shower. Every muscle in his upper body glistened wet with water and a large bath towel tied around his waist. Beads of water rolled down his eight-pack into the edge of the towel where the bulged of his penis was in plain view. She knew what was under that towel and deep inside she wanted to snatch it off, push him back on the bed, and ride it until her stomach muscles started to hurt. "But I can't do that we have company coming." she thought to herself gazing at her husband in his towel.

"What's wrong with you?" asked Sean sarcastically. "You act like you never seen a nigga in a towel before."

"Just get dressed." she said as she walks over to give him a kiss and smacks him on the ass then turns and walks back downstairs.

It had been almost a week and a half and there was still no word fro Jasper about the investigation of Bruce and Carl. Today was the day he was suppose to bring the information that he had gathered and researched with the legal assistance of Rico's office. Michelle was going to meet the two men at Rico's office when she got a call from Evette and Janet. They also wanted to go along with her, after all it did concern their family member too. Evette was very concerned and worried about her little brother, but now was the time to find out the truth. Or so they hoped. They were completely silent as the elevator reached the floor of Rico's law firm. As the doors opened their breaths were the only motion around and then they exited the elevator in what seemed like slow motion.

"Hello." a receptionist greeted them at a front counter. "May I help you?"

"Yes." Evette replied. "We're here to see Rico."

"Just a minute." she said as she pressed the talk button on the intercom system. "Sir, there is someone here to see you."

"Send them in." Rico responded.

"Come on in ladies and have a seat." said Jasper as he opens a manila folder.

"So, what did you find out?" asked Michelle.

I really didn't find out much." said Jasper. "They covered their tracks real well. I found no trace of them on any flight manifest and nothing at any of the travel agencies. Now this could be one of two possible answers, they are traveling under fake names or maybe they never left Alaska. The first thing I did when you asked me to look into this was to run a check

103

on Bruce's plates. My friends in law enforcement can only contact me if his car shows up somewhere in Alaska or at the Canadian border, but that's all. He can't be picked up or arrested because setting your wife up for adultery or conspiring with her suppose lover is not a crime. I figured he would have to have Carl with him in court to testify that he was having an affair with Michelle or so we thought. You see that's where things get tricky. Rico, maybe you should handle this one."

"Well there is no easy way to put this." Rico said hesitating to speak.

"Rico, this is not the time." inserted Evette. "Just spit it out. We've been waiting on y'all for two weeks now."

"Just to bluntly put it out there." Rico started to say. "Michelle can't get a damn dime, but the trip about it all is that Carl doesn't fit the equation at all."

"What do you mean?" strongly asked Janet. You can hear the thirst for revenge on Carl in her every breath.

"He was involved with the whole thing, how could he not be in the equation."

"Yeah, that's what we thought at first." replied Rico. "But as far as Michelle getting anything out of it, Carl is totally out of the picture. You see, we didn't find anything you can get from him because Bruce doesn't have anything."

"What are you talking about Rico?" Michelle asks. "You know as well as anybody does that Bruce has had those stores in the malls for years and all those apartment building."

"There's only one way to say this, so I'll just tell you." Rico says taking a deep breath. "I found out that all of Bruce's businesses and real estate is in Sean's name. Nobody can touch it, not even Bruce."

"What kind of shit is this Rico?" Evette asked promptly. Her eyes instantly turned bloodshot with fury and rage. "I'm gonna kill him!" she screams as she jumps out of her seat and headed for the door.

"Calm down." said Rico. "Just calm down."

"Fuck you Rico!" grunted Evette. "Don't tell me to calm down!"

"No Evette." responded Jasper. "Rico is right. Let's not jump to any conclusions until we find out the truth and the whole story before we go accusing people of shit. We haven't heard Sean's side of this story y..."

"Jasper you kiss my ass too!" interrupted Evette. "I have heard off I need to hear." she then turned and stormed out of the office slamming the door behind her.

"I don't understand." sobbed Michelle. "Why would Bruce have everything in Sean's name?"

"Well I think it's safe to say that he did it just in case things every went bad." said Jasper. "He would make sure you couldn't take nothing."

"So what about Carl?" cried Janet.

"Look ladies." inserted Rico. "Y'all should just chill out for a while and a as soon as we find out more, we'll keep you informed.

Meanwhile Evette was speeding across town, darting in and out of traffic on her way back home. She had to get to the bottom of this once and for all. How could Sean be involved in all of this mess, she thought. He can't have all that stuff in his name and not know about it. So why did he keep it a secret even from his wife? Maybe he was doing it as a favor for Bruce, but why didn't he say anything about it. Or maybe Sean himself was the mastermind to all this madness. But what did

Sean have to gain from the demise of Bruce and Michelle's marriage and what did Carl get out of all this? Her mind was racing a hundred miles an hour as she finally pulls up into her driveway. She took deep breathes in an attempt to try and calm herself as she opens the front door. It didn't work.

"Sean!" screams as she slams the door.

"I'm upstairs." Sean replied in a muffled voice. "What is it?"

"Just stay there I'm coming up there." Evette says in a distort voice as she storms up the stairs to their bedroom and bursts through the door.

"What the fuck is your problem?" immediately asked Sean.

"So when did we start keeping secrets from each other Sean?" she blurts out.

"What are you talking about?" asked Sean. "If this is about that trip to Japan, I was going to surprise you, but I can see Sharon talks too much."

"Baby." Evette replied in a calm voice. "When were you going to tell me that all of Bruce's estates are in your name?"

"I wasn't gonna tell you!" Sean responded quickly jumping into defense. "Didn't know it was such a big concern of yours. Besides it's not like you tell me everything you do. Who told you about that anyway?"

"It doesn't matter who told me." Evette screams as she starts to cry. "It wasn't you an that's the problem. And what do you mean that you wasn't gonna tell me anything. We're suppose to be married, you act like we're total strangers."

"Woman, you must be crazy." said Sean. "This is suppose to be something between me and my best friend, maybe you just wasn't suppose to know. What's so wrong with that?"

"I'm your fucking wife and even I don't know!" yelled Evette. "You don't see nothing wrong with that!"

"You need to calm the fuck down!" bluntly inserted Sean. "And lower your damn voice in my house."

"Your house." Evette responded calmly. "Your house, you can stop right there mister. I'm not like Michelle, I know for a fact that all this shit is in my name as well as yours, so don't try me. You can't claim this is your house; this is our house for our kids and us. So you need to calm down cause I'm the one that's pissed off."

"Are you threatening me?" asked Sean in a lot, but serious voice. "Because I can make threats too sister. I don't need no wife that keep accusing me of shit and snooping around behind my back."

"So what?" Evette replied with tears and pure anger in her eyes. "You gonna try to divorce me now? Go right ahead just try because I don't need no husband that hides shit from me."

"It makes me wonder what else you're hiding, another family or something. I was just trying to find out what happened to my brother and when rocks started to get turned over, my husband crawls from under one. And you want to point the finger at me, nigga fuck you! I'll tell you what. If you want a divorce just don't forget that half of all that shit is mine."

"You just don't understand baby, I love you!" responded Sean in an attempt to calm the situation. "I just want you to trust me, I don't wanna lose you. I'm in love with you."

"Love my ass!" Evette growled showing that she wasn't affected by his attempt to charm her. "You have fucked up this time. You have disrespected our marriage and my trust in you. So until the judge says you can have half of this house, it's me and my kids house, so you can get the fuck out."

"But baby you don't under..." SMACK! Sean started to say as he was interrupted by Evette's hand to his face.

"Sean, you just need to get your things and leave." Evette said giving him the look knowing that he wouldn't dare hit her back.

"I'll leave, but you're going to regret this shit." Sean says as he turns and walks away.

"Oh, so you're just gonna leave!" cried out Evette.

"I'm not gonna stay here and argue with you or give you the chance to put your hands on my face again." Sean responded. But he knows that her licks can't hurt his bulky, muscular frame, it's principle.
"If you walk out that door, it's over." Evette said. "It wont be no coming back."

Sean doesn't reply, he just turns and walks out the door. He knew that a response would only fuel the fire. Although he did have a secret involved in Bruce's businesses, Sean didn't know anything about what Carl and Bruce had going on. Bruce had kept it from everyone, even him. But at this point he felt that Evette would never accept the truth. He only did a favor for a friend, it wasn't meant to disrespect Evette. She wasn't suppose to find out because it really didn't concern her. Besides he didn't know about everything she was involved in. He knew Evette had her day spa on the East-side, but she could easily have other business ventures that he wasn't aware of. His only business was his half ownership of a logging company that he actually had to go work at four months of the year. That and his underground activities with Bruce, but he didn't have any involvement with Bruce's legitimate business venture. Bruce just used his name for a front, but this didn't mean anything to Sean. He was fed up with Evette not trusting him. They both could sense that an end to their marriage is near and Sean knew he was going to need a good lawyer. Unlike Michelle, Evette was a lot more resourceful; he also knew that she would get everything she got coming to her and then some.

ENEMY OF MY ENEMY

It had been a whole month since Sean and Evette had separated and there were still no sign of what happened to Bruce and Carl. Melissa was still pissed at Duane, Paul had yet another new drama queen of a girlfriend and no one heard from Evon since she left for Seattle. The once strong family unit was falling apart like a divided nation on the brink of civil war and everybody was starting to choose sides. No more humiliation and degradation, these family members and friends needed unity and salvation.

"Look, I don't want to talk about that shit right now." said Sean as he got out of the car and closed his cell phone. Jerome pulled up next to him and got out of the car.

"What's up Sean?" asked Jerome as he walked around the car to shake his hand. "You looking good."

"I'm cool." Sean replied. "What's up with you? I never get to see y'all no more."

"Man with all this crazy shit going on." says Jerome. "Don't nobody want to hang out anymore."

"Well we are here now." says Sean showing that he had no interest in talking about all the bullshit that was going on. "Most of us are here now, so let's go in there and drink up all of Rico's liquor."

"Hell yeah, you right." laughed Jerome as they went inside.

"What's up everybody?" said Sean as they walked in shaking hands with everyone. "I can smell it so let me inhale it."

"Oh yeah man." responded Duane handing Sean an already

burning blunt. "Try some of this shit."

Sean grabbed the blunt from Duane and walked over to Henry at the bar to get a drink. Sean and Jerome had just got there, but everyone else was drunk. They had to play catch up. Paul was passed out on the couch like he always does after Henry challenges him to a drink off. Rico was in the kitchen talking to Duane lying about something, but Duane didn't care, he was looking for the blunt. The same old ambiance, but something wasn't right. It was just different without Bruce and Carl. After what seemed like an eternity, but Sean was expecting it all along, someone was going to eventually drop the question.

"So, Sean." blurted out Henry. "What the fuck is on with you and Evette?"

"Man, you know. The same old shit." replied Sean. "Evette is always accusing me of different things, but this last time she went too far. She even did some investigating on me and that was the last straw. I didn't think about it at the time, but she did get all this private information on me about the same time Jasper was in town....Oh shit, that's it!"

"Let me talk to you for a second Rico." Jerome interrupted as he noticed Rico's eyes getting bigger as Sean was talking. The two men step into the back room as Sean continued talking in the living room.

"Nigga please, tell me that you didn't have nothing to do with Sean and Evette splitting up." Jerome insisted.

"What are you talking about?" nervously responded Rico.

"Don't plat that shit with me." said Jerome. "I know that look muthafucka, you know something! If you had something to do with them getting divorced, you better fix that shit right now."

"Man, it's worse than that." Rico started to sob. "Evette and

110

Michelle came to me for some help getting some information about Bruce, but it turns out she can't touch Bruce because everything is in Sean's name. I didn't know, it surprised me too. Besides Jasper was helping too, so they would have found out anyway."

"Jasper, I'm glad Sharon left his ass." replied Jerome. "But if you tell Sean I'm sure he'll understand."

"No, I told you that it was worse than that." said Rico.

"What could be worse than ruining your friend's marriage." Jerome said. "Keeping it a fucking secret."

"Evette also knows a secret on me." replied Rico. "She wants to really make Sean hurt, so I have to represent her in the divorce or my secret will come out. A secret that will destroy me and everything I have."

"Are you crazy?" asked Jerome. "What do you think Sean's gonna do when he comes to court and his home is representing his wife."

"I don't know what to do." said Rico. "This shit is getting out of control."

"Well, you better do something." inserted Jerome. "Sean is sitting in your living room talking about the problems that you helped cause."

"You don't have to tell me nothing!" yelled Sean as he kicks in the door. "I heard the whole thing." as he walks up to Rico and starts punching him in the face. Jerome didn't try to stop it because he felt that Rico was getting what he deserved. Then all of a sudden all of the men ran to the room to break it up. Just in time for Rico because Sean was really starting to pound on him hard.

"What's going on?" yelled Henry. "Why are y'all fighting Sean, we're all family."

"Tell them Rico!" growled Sean. "Tell everybody how you plan to represent Evette in our divorce trial. Tell everybody how you are going to fuck me over."

Everyone got silent as Rico dropped his head in shame. He didn't think in a million years that it would come out like this.

"Let my fucking arm go!" said Sean. "If I really wanted to get his all y'all couldn't hold me anyway." With the entire house completely silent and the only motion around is Sean's breath. He snatches his keys from the coffee table an walked out the door.

Meanwhile, back on the hillside, Evette, Sharon and Melissa sit out on the balcony of what used to be Sean and Evette's bedroom. Now it's just Evette's house for her and her friends to come and kick it with her. In between the times when she had the kids home at her. Sean bought a new house right after they split up and the kids loved it there, so Evette didn't have then a lot. Sean gave her lots of freedom and Evette took full advantage of it.

"Girl, you know I've been doing good." said Sharon. "Since Jasper came back to town."

"Well, that's good." replied Melissa sipping on a martini that Sharon was famous for. "It's good to see things work out for somebody."
"Don't worry, everything will work out for you." said Evette. "Don't let that shit get you down."

"I don't know what I was thinking anyway." Melissa responded. "I should have known not to trust Duane, but it just kind of happened to fast and before I realized it, I had feeling for him."

"I know what you mean." said Sharon. "Jasper has been talking that shit about getting back together. I told him that he was moving too fast. Everything is cool the way it is, I don't want to trust him because I don't want to get hurt. Men don't care about your feelings, it's in their nature. Now don't get me wrong, some of them are cool to kick it with and have around, but you shouldn't be catching feelings for them. Especially not nobody like Duane."

"Yeah, I still feel guilty for keeping it a secret from everybody." said Melissa. "And Duane is acting like it never happened."

"Fuck him!" Evette said with a blunt seriousness in her voice. "Girl you can move on, don't even trip over that shit."

"So you mean to tell me that you wouldn't take Sean back if he asked you?" asked Sharon smacking her lips with sarcasm.

"Hell no." Evette responded. "He and I have grown apart over the years and this whole break up is a validation of how far apart we've gotten. I just felt that all his secrets were going to unfold and I didn't want to stick around and get hurt. So exactly what Sharon was telling you I agree with her because if you don't want to get hurt you have to look out for your own feelings. A man wouldn't give a fuck how you felt or even care about stepping all over your feelings."

Just as the three women were elaborating on the evil in the hearts of men, the doorbell ringing interrupted them. Evette immediately goes downstairs to answer it. As she opens the door, in rushes Jasper breathing heavy as if he had ran all the way there. Hearing all the commotion downstairs, Sharon and Melissa also came to see what was going on.

"What's going on?" asked Evette with a curious frown on her face.

"I came here as fast as I could." blurted out Jasper panting heavily. "I had to make sure that y'all were okay."

"See if we're okay?" Sharon inserted with a look of confusion.

"What is this shit all about?" asked Evette. "Pull yourself together man, you act like child support is chasing your ass or something."

"Rico just called me." replied Jasper. "Sean found out everything and jumped on Rico. He's probably on his way here now. We gotta get out of here. And if he's on to Rico, I'm sure he knows about me helping you out finding all that information on him. Man I need a drink!"

"Nigga, are you crazy!" inserted Evette as she opens the door suggesting that Jasper get out. "I don't know about you and Rico, but nobody here is scared of Sean."

"Evette is right." said Sharon standing by Evette's side. "Be a fucking man, you come over here all out of breath and scared not to protect us, but you want us to run like you. Fuck you Jasper. Oh yeah. The answer is no, I don't want to get back with you coming over here acting like a punk. So I guess you need to go back to Texas alone and call me when you want to see your son."

At the same time Sean was pulling up in front of the law offices of Mya Winslow. Mya was Evette's cousin that has always competed against her since they were kids. Always arguing and fighting with each other at family reunions and gathering. They had one last big fight their sophomore year of college and haven't spoken to each other since. Family or not, Mya despised Evette and Evette felt the same way about her. But why was an enraged Sean going to her office although she always talked to Sean, Evette never knew about it. Sean always thought of their fight with each other as being stupid. Mya was just as beautiful and jazzy as Evette, but Sean didn't look at her like that. There was no way he could convince her to talk to Evette, so what was he trying to accomplish by going to see her. As he entered the building he approached a young receptionist at the front desk.

"Hello, may I help you?" the young lady asked as she looked Sean up and down with sexual interest.

"Yes." Sean replied. "I'm here to see Ms. Winslow and I don't have an appointment, but just tell her it's Sean, she will see me."

"Ms. Winslow, there's a Sean here to see you." said the receptionist with no response from Mya.

"Hey kinfolk." Mya said as she walks out of her office to hug and greet him. "What brings you by?"

"Can we talk in private?" Sean asked.

"Sure." she said as she walks Sean back into her office and closed the door. "What can I help you with?"

"Well I'm sure you've heard." Sean started to explain. "Me and Evette split up. She has been talking all this shit about taking the kids and everything from me. She just keeps insisting on making this divorce messy. Then I over heard Rico saying he was going to represent Evette in my divorce. I don't know what she is trying to do getting my friend to go against me, but it's some dirty shit."

"No need to say anymore." as Mya stopped him short in mid sentence. "You know I', a criminal lawyer, but a chance to get back at that bitch is so sweet I can taste it. Sean, I would love to take this case."

They both just smiled, as they didn't say another word.

THE END BOOK 1

Born and raised in Texas until the age of 16. I joined the U.S. Army at 16 and was stationed at Ft. Richardson, Alaska. At age 17, while on active duty, I received my high school diploma and started taking my college courses at the University of Alaska Anchorage. After three years in the army, I returned to Texas to fi nish my degree at North Texas State. Although my major wasn't in literature. I still have amazing story telling abilities that are more than obvious in my works. I constantly strive for greatness in my writing as each book that I publish gets better and more amazing than the one before it.